MURDER AT THE OASIS CLUB

Totally Addictive Cozy Murder Mystery

Massachusetts Cozy Mystery
Book 9

ANDREA KRESS

Chapter 1

On a cool spring morning in Beacon Hill, Mr. and Mrs. Burnside came down to the morning room for breakfast followed by their elder daughter, Amanda. Their younger daughter, Louisa, was habitually the last to arrive. The morning paper was laid out for the head of the household to read during the meal, and the noise of snapping open the pages alerted the maid, Simona, who was in the kitchen, that the family was ready to be served.

"Good morning, sir, missus," she said bringing in a platter of French toast, one of the family's favorites since Cook always used the highest quality white bread. She set the plate down for them to serve themselves while she retrieved a pot of coffee from the kitchen.

Mr. Burnside grumbled as he read.

"I don't know why you subject yourself to the news first thing in the morning," his wife said. "It always makes you cross."

"If it's not one thing, it's another. Europe is starting up all the old grudges. As if the Great War wasn't enough to sober mankind into eternal peace! Here we go again."

"It's not that bad Daddy, is it?" Amanda asked.

"The markets are going to be volatile. Germany has been doing so badly they are itching for a fight. I just hope they don't mean all that saber rattling literally."

"Put the paper down, dear, and enjoy your meal."

"Yes, good idea. I haven't even got to the national news to see what's going on in Washington, much less the latest here in Boston."

Amanda had taken the pages dealing with local issues and, after a few paragraphs, said, "I don't understand why they bother to write about a rise in crime and blame it on gangs without saying where their information came from. Why are they so vague?"

"Good point. Maybe nobody wants to admit being the source. Surely not the Mayor's office, even if they track such a thing. The last thing he wants is to be blamed for crime or the causes of it. Using the term 'gangs' makes it seem as if there are shadowy, mysterious groups who are responsible for bad things happening. Perhaps gangs *are* responsible. In that case, no reporter in his right mind would identify who those organized groups are. That would be the end of him."

"Oh, Edward, let's talk about something more pleasant," Mrs. Burnside said.

"Morning, all," Louisa said, breezing into the room. "French toast! My favorite."

"What are you up to today?" her mother asked. Since Louisa worked as a designer at an upscale women's clothing salon, she always had a tidbit of gossip or a name to drop that intrigued her mother.

"Some new women appeared the other day and I hate to say it, but they seemed out of their element."

"In what way?"

"This is going to sound horribly snobbish, but they were dressed badly."

"I should think that is your ideal customer. At least they knew to go there and you're just the young woman to steer them in the right direction," her father said.

"It was odd that, as we were discussing the type of dresses she would be interested in ordering, the younger woman searched in her handbag muttering about having the money with her. Anyone would know that we send an invoice after the work is done."

"I'm sure you will school them properly," her mother said.

"And all of a sudden, she pulls out what can only be described as a giant wad of bills held together with a rubber band! My eyes must have popped out of my head."

Her parents laughed at the image.

"Mother, you hardly ever ask about what my day will be like," Amanda said, pretending to be offended.

"I'm sorry, dear. I still don't know what it is that you do."

"She peeks through keyholes and spies on people," Louisa said.

"That's hardly the job description of a private investigator," Mr. Burnside said. "And the work she's been doing for our firm, assisting with research, has been invaluable."

"This week is tracking down paperwork for one of the partner's cases. It requires concentration and focus, things that I'm good at."

"Oh, well, we can't all be boring," Louisa said with a smile.

"Girls," her mother said, shaking her head although she knew their teasing was mild.

Mr. Burnside pushed his plate aside and perused the section of the paper that Amanda had abandoned. "Would you look at that! I don't know what the Mayor thinks he is doing, but it's not keeping law and order. 'Suspected gang activity.' Can you imagine? What's that fiancé of yours doing to protect us from these villains?" he asked Amanda.

"From what Brendan says, there has always been gang activity in Boston. The men take a pledge to be quiet about what they do and they cover for each other with alibis if they're arrested. The people who run them change from time to time, but they do the same nasty things," Amanda said.

"I'm worried about you, young lady," Mr. Burnside said to Louisa, whose boyfriend owned the Oasis nightclub. "That type of person seems to like to hang out in taverns and clubs. I think you should restrict your attendance there to no more than two nights a week."

Louisa pouted and looked to her mother for support. "I get to show off my designs and make connections with women and that brings in business for Monsieur Josef. And as far as I know, Rob doesn't allow gangsters in his place."

"Not that you know of," her father muttered.

After a hesitation she said brightly, "Speaking of Brendan, have you set a date yet?"

"Were we speaking of Brendan?" Amanda asked, knowing her sister was anxious to get the spotlight off herself. "For your information, we're going to discuss it over dinner tonight. Lots of things to consider."

"Such as?" her sister asked.

"Large or small—"

"Catholic service or our church," Louisa finished.

Amanda let out a breath. "Yes, that is something critical to consider. We may enter negotiations on that this evening."

Mr. and Mrs. Burnside exchanged looks while Amanda pretended not to notice.

If they thought that the religious differences between the two were the only obstacle in the family's way, they had another thing coming.

Chapter 2

"Your father is so kind to always offer me a glass of sherry when I come by," Brendan said, squeezing Amanda's hand before putting the car into gear and pulling away from the curb.

"Don't your parents have a pre-dinner drink?" she asked, surprised that she had never noticed or thought to ask before.

"My father will have a beer with dinner and that's about it. With the chaos of so many people in the household, my mother has got to keep her wits about her."

"She certainly juggles a lot, what with Bridie and the baby and your brother-in-law as several more mouths to feed."

"It has been a strange thing for him and for the family. But there has been a new development. Employment!"

"That's wonderful. It had to have been demoralizing to be out of work so long. Where is he going to be?" Amanda asked.

"He's going to be a bookkeeper for Rob Worley."

"What? At the Oasis?"

"Sure. Clubs need to keep financial records. How much of their reporting is above board is not my concern."

Amanda turned to look at him as he focused his gaze ahead, paying attention to the traffic.

"What does that mean, exactly?"

Brendan regretted having made the comment but felt obliged to explain. "Some businesses take inventory of discrete things—like shoes or cars. But when you're dealing with food and alcohol, counting how many drinks or steaks are sold can be less accurate."

"What are you getting at?"

"Not to suggest that Rob and his backer José are doing this, but many people in the food and drink industry tend to fudge when it comes to declaring income. And it's easier when you have a bar or a restaurant."

"To minimize sales tax or income tax?"

"Yes, both. It's not unusual for the owners of those kinds of businesses to downplay their daily deposits by pocketing some of the cash at the end of the night."

"Oh," she said, puzzled that he knew about such things.

"When you go into a regular store and pay, they ring you up at the cash register, right? When is the last time you heard the 'ting' of a cash register at the Oasis? An interesting thing I learned was that pricing things at ninety-nine cents instead of a dollar is done because everyone likes to think that they're getting a bargain.

Ninety-nine cents seems so much less expensive than a dollar. But that pricing has another benefit. It makes the person at the register ring up the sale to give the customer change. That way the owner knows when a sale is being made. Otherwise, that person could just pocket the dollar and the owner would be none the wiser." He winked at her.

"Do you think Rob and José are doing that?" she asked.

He shrugged his shoulders. "I bet they don't handle direct sales themselves. Here we are," he said as they pulled up in front of Catalano's in the North End, the restaurant they considered 'their place.'

The owner, Mr. Russo, greeted them effusively, not only as steady customers but because his daughter Simona had found a position as a maid in the Burnside home. They all knew she was capable of more than that, but times were still tough as far as employment was concerned, and it was a comfortable position with the benefit of easy-going employers, a light workload and the meals that Cook provided as part of the package.

Mr. Russo took their coats and showed them to a booth where they could have the private conversation that he knew the engaged couple was looking forward to. While they sat down, he announced that his wife had made her spectacular osso bucco for that evening and it was highly recommended.

"Shall we?" Brendan asked her and she nodded, not sure what it was except something that the proprietor was proud of.

Wine was ordered and bread arrived as Amanda wondered how they would tackle the conversation.

"So," she began and then stopped. "What would you like to decide first? The date?"

"All right. That sounds easy. What about June?" he asked.

"That is the traditional month. Which means it is also the busiest month and reservations may already be in short supply."

"Really? Do people actually plan that far in advance?"

"Yes, Brendan. It is considered one of life's more important occasions," she said.

The bottle of Chianti arrived and Mr. Russo poured it for them and nodded.

They toasted, took a sip and Brendan cleared his throat. "All right, then, what would you suggest?"

"I didn't mean that June was out of the question, just that securing a church and the reception location might be difficult."

"Perhaps we should tackle the thorniest thing first."

Amanda bristled. "And what would that be?"

"You know very well. Whose church?"

"Obviously, my parents would prefer it to be at Trinity Church."

"And mine would like it to be at the Cathedral of the Holy Cross."

They were quiet for a moment.

"I may have more weight to my argument seeing as my brother is a priest and would love to perform the ceremony," Brendan said.

"That's hardly fair. I don't have any brothers or relatives who are in the clergy to my knowledge. What if I scrounged around the family tree and produced a minister?"

Before Brendan could reply, Mr. Russo brought out two plates of the osso bucco, with carrots poking out of the dark gravy. They thanked him profusely and tucked in.

"Now, not to be argumentative, but don't you think that the choice of church should relate to the degree of attachment to either the church or the religion?"

"What do you mean by that?" Amanda asked warily.

"Well, not that you don't take your beliefs seriously, but I would assert that Roman Catholics have had more investment and obligations than other forms of Christianity."

Amanda stared at him. "What a preposterous thing to say!"

"It's true. We are required to attend Mass every Sunday and don't eat meat on Friday."

"I am sure I've seen you eat a meat sandwich on a Friday."

"Naturally there are exceptions, such as when one has to work or only meat is available," Brendan said, looking down at his plate.

"That's a slim excuse."

"And we have a rigorous, extensive course in religious instruction from first grade all the way to confirmation at age twelve. We must memorize questions and answers for the catechism and the lives of the saints and are tested on them. We don't get the easy path of attending Sunday School where you get read Bible stories."

"We have confirmation, too, you know."

"I bet you didn't get slapped in the face by a bishop to affirm your commitment to stand firm for your religion," Brendan countered.

"That didn't happen," Amanda challenged him.

"It certainly did. The nuns told us that he would tap us on the cheek and that's what they did in our many rehearsals. Then the day came and he walloped each and every one of us."

Amanda began to laugh.

"And the nuns—oh, I didn't give you the lowdown on the nuns who carried rulers and not for measurement purposes. It was to smack you on the hand if you talked out of turn or misbehaved. It was less painful than what the brothers did when we were older. They usually had a cricket bat, so you dared not step out of line."

"Now you're making that up," she said.

He held up his hand. "I will swear to it on a stack of Bibles."

"The amount of suffering you endured as a child and adult due to your religion's requirements does not give you the upper hand in deciding where we are going to be married."

"We could always elope," he said. "Pocket the presents and save your family a lot of money."

"Bren. No."

"Changing the subject, this dish is delicious. It must have been cooking half the day," he said.

They ate in silence for a few minutes.

"Changing the subject back," Amanda began. "Isn't there some requirement about the spouse converting?"

"Ah, now we do hit a sticking point. There is no rule about you having to convert, although you are welcome to do so. It is widely known that converts are the most conscientious of Catholics."

"I'll take it under consideration," she said.

"The requirement is that the children must be brought up Roman Catholic."

"I suppose that wouldn't be the most difficult of concessions. Except, of course, that the Catholic father would be the one to supervise the religious studies, ferry the children to their catechism classes and weekly worship and arrange for the First Communion outfits and celebrations and the same for their confirmation."

"That's quite an obligation."

"Fair's fair," she said.

"Let's slip onto an easier decision. Will it be June or some other month, elopement being off the table."

"June will suit. My mother will be delighted to make the arrangements."

"Reception—where?"

"Again, my mother will take care of that. Whatever is available will dictate the time of day for the event. Maid of honor, Louisa, of course. And I'll have to think hard about the bridesmaids. Who will be your best man?"

"That's a good one. Can't be Patrick. But what if he officiates along with the minister of your choice?"

"Has that ever been done?" she asked.

"I have no idea. And I don't know if either church would acquiesce to having a double officiants."

"Why do things have to be so difficult?" she asked, suddenly saddened by the complexity of what should be a straightforward decision.

Brendan reached across the table and took her hand. "Maybe elopement or a civil ceremony is not such a bad idea."

"So, two families can be disappointed in us?"

"The best solution I have right now is to stop thinking about the obstacles and just enjoy our dinner. Perhaps by letting it sit, the solution will present itself."

Amanda sighed, not seeing a clear resolution and wondering how to talk to her parents about the issue.

Chapter 3

The next day, Brendan was busy working on detective assignments for the upcoming week when Herb put his head around the door.

"Mr. Symington to see you," he said.

"Jeez, I'm busy," Brendan said.

"He wanted to meet with the Chief and I couldn't do that. He's your buddy, isn't he?" Herb said with a smirk.

"Okay, okay, I'll go out and escort him in." He got up with a weary sigh and made his way out to the reception area where the small man with the intense look and brush moustache stood up to greet him.

"How are you today, Mr. Symington?"

"Not well. Things are going very badly."

"Let's wait until we get into my office and we can talk about it."

As they approached his office, Brendan turned and said to him, "I have a staff meeting in half an hour so we'll need to keep this brief."

Mr. Symington hustled to keep up and, once in his office, Brendan closed the door.

"What can I help you with?" he asked, although he knew what the conversation would be about since they had had it before. "Please sit down."

"It's these clubs. Now, when Prohibition was in force, those illegal taverns, bars and clubs knew to keep their noses clean—at least as far as the public was concerned. Since the Eighteenth Amendment was repealed, it's been the Wild West out there."

"How do you mean?" Brendan asked, despite knowing the line of reasoning from the man who had made the same complaint several times before.

"There are stipulated hours of operation for establishments that serve alcohol." He had his usual stack of papers with him and paged through them, looking for the wording he sought and not finding it. "It's very specific, but the hoodlums who own and operate these places pay no attention to what closing hours are supposed to be. They may be open twenty-four hours a day for all I know. My question again is: what are you going to do about it?"

"Mr. Symington, I've explained to you before that there are two levels of jurisdiction relating to businesses that sell alcohol. First, a person must apply to the Alcohol Beverage Control Commission for a license to sell alcohol. They check the background of the applicant first."

"Sure! If you've got a conviction, you can't be the person of record. So, you get a straw man to apply."

"That may be so, but it is not in the Boston Police Department's remit to check or challenge that. It is the Commission that must do that."

"They don't seem to care! They say they have several inspectors, but I've never seen them at work and you never read about infractions in the newspaper."

"Do you have a specific establishment for which you would like to lodge a complaint?"

"I have several," the man said, shuffling through his pile of papers.

"Then that information should go to the ABC Commission, not to us."

"I've called them. I've gone in person and they won't let me speak at their meetings, which are supposedly open to the public. Sure, open meeting, but they don't want to hear from you. Why would they? They get money from the licensing and a percentage of alcohol sales in the state. It's in their best interest to maintain a distance."

"I believe the Commissioners are appointed by the Governor and have no financial interest in how many licenses are granted or how much money flows into the state."

"Maybe not directly. But they are indebted to the Governor for giving them the status of being a Commissioner. And he is indebted to them for not making waves but making sure the state's coffers are full. You know, you scratch my back, and I'll scratch yours."

Brendan took a deep breath. They had had almost the same exchange several weeks earlier but logic was not winning the day.

"Cities and towns have a hand in licensing, too. They can deny a license based upon the proximity to a school or church," Brendan said.

"I know that. That's not the issue. The problem is them staying open longer than they are supposed to."

"Have you talked to your Councilman about this?"

Symington huffed. "Are you joking? Those guys are happy to stop into any bar, tavern or club in the city and get a free drink. Why would they want to disrupt that happy arrangement? Besides, I've seen with my own eyes the Mayor barhopping, as they call it."

That was a new argument added to their usual exchange.

"What do you mean?"

"He'll start the evening at one place, then move on to one or two more before going home."

Brendan paused. "Have you been following him?"

Symington hesitated. "Not in that sense. I was out walking one night and saw his car pull up to the front door of a fancy club. They made a big fuss about him being there. The guy who parks the cars welcomed him and the Mayor knew his name. I don't doubt Hizzoner got at least one free drink for his patronage. And another thing, as a citizen, I don't like it that the man who runs our city is out till all hours. Probably drunk!"

"That's quite an accusation, sir."

"Well, it's true. If people knew…they'd be very worried. Coming in with a hangover the next day while making big decisions. You should be worried, too," he said, jabbing an index finger in Brendan's direction.

"Maybe the City needs to work with the Commission to pass the information along to them and that would make a difference."

"That's a good idea," Symington said.

"It's a political and managerial decision that can't be made or implemented by me, however," Brendan said.

Symington stood up. "I can see you're not going to be of any help." He moved to the door and turned. "Does someone have to get killed before you all take any action?" He stormed out of the room.

Herb, who must have been nearby, came in.

"Everything all right, boss?"

"No."

"Do you want us to keep an eye on him?"

"No. He's frustrated and, unfortunately, the system that's in place has no remedy for his complaints."

Herb grunted. "Everyone's got an axe to grind." He gestured with his thumb and said, "We're ready for the staff meeting."

Chapter 4

At City Hall, the Mayor was having his own staff meeting to review the material on the agenda for the Council meeting later that day. His longtime secretary, Mrs. Derwin, had asked the son of one of the Mayor's friends, who was acting as a six-month intern, to cover the phones at the reception desk while they had their closed-door meeting. Mrs. Derwin was at the ready with her stenographer's notebook, not to record the discussions of the meeting but to make note of and schedule any meetings or calls that arose from their discussions. She began with reminding him of important milestones—births, marriages or deaths—among his constituents for which a note from the Mayor would be appreciated and remembered.

The youthful-looking Henry Rogers, who accompanied the Mayor on most of his official business, sat nearby without need of notebook or pen and paper as his memory and recall were sufficient for any task. Paul Mooney, one of the Mayor's oldest friends, was in charge of constituent services and had little business with the legislative functions of the Council meetings. However, he was present in the event a member of the public had expressed an opinion on upcoming ordinances.

The key person for each staff meeting was the disheveled Bill Flagg, with his preoccupied air and scuffed bulging briefcase. He plopped it on the empty chair to his right and pulled out the thick notebook that contained the day's agenda material and another stack of lined sheets with his notes.

"Ready, Mrs. D?" the Mayor asked as he sat back in his chair.

She read through a long list of names whom she thought he might want to acknowledge with a card, a congratulatory letter or flowers in the event of a death. He nodded throughout until she came to one recently deceased person and he shook his head.

"Good riddance," he said, and she drew a line through it.

"That's all, sir." She sat back and all eyes were on Bill Flagg, who had been shuffling through his notes.

"Bill."

"The consent agenda looks fine."

"Paul, anybody contact us registering objections?"

"Nope."

"Good. Go on."

"Appointments to the following Boards," he said handing a sheet of paper to the Mayor.

"Most of them have spoken to you, so Mrs. Derwin has told me. All okay?"

"Yes. And I particularly like that we have an Italian nominee. We need to embrace the people. He's a good guy, from what I hear. Henry, what do you pick up from the other Council Members? Okay with him or not?"

"They seem fine. He's not one to rock the boat."

"Good."

"The rezonings have been vetted through the Development Office and seem airtight," Bill said.

"Not a peep from anyone," Paul said. "To my knowledge."

That qualifier pulled everyone's attention in his direction.

"We're good," he said, holding up both hands.

"Liquor licenses have passed through the ABC Commission process and our own licensing process without a hitch. Only two this time."

"Good."

Paul and Henry looked at one another, with the younger one deferring to the elder.

"It's not a large contingent, but a noisy one that wants us to have tighter control on licenses," Paul said.

"How? We're following the law," the Mayor said.

"Yes, but this small group thinks that drink is evil, destroys families, you know."

"We've got a Carrie Nation in our midst?" She was a figure from the past evoking furious women breaking into saloons and smashing the furniture and bottles with an axe. That provoked some laughter. "Prohibition is over! It's been over! It's in the City's best interests to encourage business, not stand in its way. Why shouldn't a few folks benefit from alcohol sales? Let's spread the wealth."

"That's just the tip of the iceberg. There's something buried in another item which stipulates that the closing hours of," and here Bill flipped through the pages in front of him to get the correct wording. "'*The closing hours of all establishments providing spirituous liquors be changed to midnight.*'"

"What!" the Mayor thundered. "That's absurd! People are just getting going on a weekend at that time. Who the hell put this on the agenda?"

"I think you know," Henry said.

"What are you hearing from folks, Paul?"

"Nothing except the group I mentioned just now."

They looked at each other.

"Council Member Carmichael is the one who proposed it," Henry said.

"That moron!" the Mayor scoffed.

"He's got a coalition of religious leaders who are in support of it. I saw one of them come out of his office this morning. They're trying to keep it on the down low and pack the audience with supporters."

"That son of a—." The Mayor stopped short in deference to Mrs. Derwin, who had heard worse from him. "Take it off the agenda."

The staff members looked at each other, recognizing how irregular that was with the meeting only hours away. The Mayor knew that as well, but he wasn't having it.

"We have to do that by majority vote," Henry said.

The Mayor glared at him. Then he looked at Mrs. Derwin. Call the Clerk and tell him I want to see him immediately. No excuses!"

The meeting was done and the staff scattered to their small, shared office off the reception room but left the door open. They waited until they heard the weary footsteps of the Clerk approach Mrs. Derwin's desk.

"Go right in, he's waiting for you," she said in her usual cheerful voice.

Somewhat relieved, he went in with the hope that the matter was trivial. Instead, he was met by a blast from the Mayor, who had been standing.

"What's the meaning of this added paragraph in item five?"

"Sorry?" the Clerk asked.

The Mayor came from behind his desk and pointed to the page where the innocuous item was printed and pointed his index finger at the paragraph about spirituous liquors.

"I don't know." The Clerk was aghast. "That's not what was signed off by the City Attorney or me."

"Yet his signature and yours are on the next page."

"Someone substituted this new page," the Clerk insisted.

The Mayor tore the page out of his notebook. "Where are the other Council Members' notebooks?"

"Up in my office."

The Mayor looked at the clock on the wall over the door. "You have exactly three hours to create a substitute page—which was the original page—and make sure there are enough copies for all the Councilors, me, yourself and the City Attorney. And replace those pages before the meeting begins. Do you understand?"

The Clerk nodded and scurried out with the page in his hand. He had enough staff to retype the page without the rogue language and replace the pages in the three-ring binders that were used by the elected officials. But he had to swear the staff to silence about the matter as he and they would surely come under fire after the fact by whoever had perpetrated the ruse in the first place.

The Clerk took the stairs down to his office rather than waiting for the elevator and wasting even a minute's time. He burst through the door of his office where ten women were busy new filing new requests that had come in that morning.

"Stop everything. Don't let anyone in. There's been an illegal action taken and I don't know how it happened. Someone replaced a page of the agenda material without my knowledge and we must rectify the situation."

The women looked at one another in shock. This sort of thing had never happened before to their knowledge.

"This is the sheet. All that needs to be retyped is the first two paragraphs. Do not, I repeat, do not include that last paragraph about spirituous liquors. Understood? Millie, Doris, Patsy, tear out the sheets and distribute them to the others. We'll get this done in no time."

Although the Mayor had suggested that it would be difficult to complete the task in the allotted time, the Clerk knew that his girls, as he called them, incredibly fast typists, could complete all copies in less than an hour. Once he checked them over, had the holes punched and sheets replaced, he would get to the matter of who was responsible.

He stood in the room while they loaded their typewriters with paper and the loud clacking of the machines began as they got to work. The Clerk walked amongst their stations, not because he thought they needed any close supervision, but because he thought he might be able to detect a guilty look.

He pulled Millie, who was supervising the operation, into his own office. He sat down and left her standing.

"Do you have any idea how this happened?"

"No, sir. It's rare that anybody is left alone in the office."

"When did the girls load up the books?"

"Yesterday. We always do it a day before the meeting."

The Clerk pinched his lower lip between his thumb and first knuckle. "What happened yesterday?"

Millie shrugged, looking bewildered and fearing for her job.

"A fire drill. Remember?" he asked.

"Yes, but…"

"Anybody could have come in here while we were scrambling down the stairs, thinking it could be the real thing."

She put her hand to her mouth.

"Did you account for all the girls when you got outside?"

"Well, no. The Fire Chief was in the main lobby and told us it was just a drill because so many of us were terrified that it might be a real fire. He had a stopwatch in his hand to time how long it would take for the building to be emptied. We stood around just outside, wondering how long it might take."

"And I'll bet he didn't have his firemen check every office of every floor to make sure nobody was left behind," he said mostly to himself.

"I don't know."

"Keep your eyes peeled. It could have been one of the girls."

"Oh, surely not," Millie protested.

"Or maybe someone's boyfriend. Or maybe someone got paid to do this."

The frown lines on Millie's forehead deepened. "Do you think we have to lock up the meeting books from now on? How can we possibly know if something has been altered without looking through every page in each book?"

"I don't know the answer to who did this. But we may have to increase security somehow. Limit who has keys to the office. And yes, lock up the meeting books. Otherwise, heads will roll, and mine is not going to be the one!"

THE GIRLS GOT the replacement pages done and inserted into the books in plenty of time.

Aside from the item on the page that had been replaced, there was nothing of much controversy on the agenda. The audience had only a few early visitors who were representatives of the people who had brought their maps and charts for the rezoning items and who might not even be asked to make a presentation. They were familiar faces at the meetings in recent years as people rarely represented themselves in such matters anymore. Instead, they had begun to hire companies whose specialty was elegant visuals so the Councilors could easily see what was being requested.

The Clerk looked at the clock to find they were still an hour away from start time. A troop of Boy Scouts came in. Their leader approached the Clerk and introduced himself as the person who had requested that the boys attend. Smiles all around.

"I'm sure the Mayor would like to take a photo with you all."

"That would be swell," the leader, who looked like a young teacher, said.

Henry Rogers came out from a side entrance and conferred with the Clerk for a moment before approaching the troop leader.

"Would your boys like to lead in the Pledge of Allegiance?" he asked.

Both the leader and boys were wide-eyed at the honor.

There was a disturbance at the doors to the Council chambers, and Henry looked up to see more than thirty solemn people, men and women, filing into the room, one of them carrying a banner that was rolled up.

"Oh, no," Henry muttered and thought it was time to approach them with his constituent-friendly face.

"Hello, welcome to the meeting. Please sit down."

They did, with one person holding one end of the banner and another unfurling it.

SAVE OUR FAMILIES was painted in red letters on the sheet.

Henry nodded his head sagely at the wholesome message. But what had that do with anything today?

The next group seating in the same row had a banner that read: STOP LATE NIGHT DRINKING.

Henry backed away and walked calmly to the door that led to the main foyer, where he sped up and dashed to the elevator and to the Mayor's office.

"Where is he?" he asked Mrs. Derwin, who was startled at his sudden entry.

"On the phone," she answered.

Ignoring her response, he knocked on the door and entered, something the Mayor frowned upon when he was on the phone and at that moment scowled intensely.

Henry waved his arm around, miming hanging up the receiver.

"Excuse me, I have to go now." The Mayor hung up the phone. "What's the matter with you?"

"There are lot of people downstairs. They came early and they are grim-faced."

"So?"

"They're here about that rogue amendment that Carmichael slipped into the agenda. And by the looks of it, they're looking for blood."

The Council meetings were always scheduled for late afternoon so that at least some working people could attend if they needed to. But seldom was the entire lower area as well as the upper gallery full. On that day, it was standing room only, with the puzzled yet polite Boy Scouts and their leader suddenly without seats. They stood by the sidelines near the flag, which was appropriate to their task that day.

The Mayor and Henry were behind the screen that allowed people in the Council chambers anteroom to peer out at the crowd. For once, the two of them were momentarily speechless before the Mayor blurted, "Where's the Clerk?"

A solemn procession of wheeled carts was making its way down the hall leading to the antechamber behind the strained face of the Clerk. The Mayor smiled at him.

"All well?" he asked.

"Yes, indeed, Your Honor," was the reply for which he was clapped on the shoulder by the taller man.

The Mayor gestured grandly with his arm for the Clerk's staff to proceed into the chambers where they were met with the buzzing of conversation and a full house. Trained to be discreet, the only reaction was a raised eyebrow from one of the assistants as they placed the agenda books in front of each place and wheeled the carts back out through the anteroom.

Finally, after each Councilor was present, everyone stood and the Mayor introduced the Boy Scout troop to lead in the Pledge of Allegiance. That done, Father O'Rourke, one of the rotating members of the faith community, said a prayer asking for guidance and humility in conducting the affairs of the City of Boston. Some of the Councilors made the sign of the cross; they all sat down and business began.

"First, due to a request from the gentlemen making the presentation needing to attend to other business, I'd like to reorder the items on the agenda, moving item seven up to the top. Do I have a second? Yes, thank you. All in favor?"

All but two Council Members voted in favor and the two who didn't looked at one another in surprise.

"We have our consent agenda relating to minutes of the last meeting and several items relating to honoring veterans of the Great War. Would anyone like to remove something from the consent agenda?" the Mayor asked.

One Council Member raised his hand but the Mayor ignored him.

"Can I have a motion to accept the consent agenda?"

Someone said, "So moved."

"Second," came from another voice.

"All in favor?" the Mayor asked.

Everyone said 'Aye.'

"Point of order, Mayor," Carmichael said.

"Yes?" the Mayor asked.

"Why is item five the last on the agenda now?"

The Mayor gave him his most imperious look. "The majority of people present are here for that item, as I understand it. In consideration of others who have shorter presentations, and at their request, it has been moved. Item one," the Mayor intoned as Carmichael fumed in his seat.

The rezonings were presented and accepted, the Intergovernmental Agreement with the County had no discussion and full agreement by the Council, and the other items were swiftly voted upon. Shortly before they got to the item for which the crowd was assembled, Carmichael flipped to that page in their book and saw that the language had been changed back to the original. He looked over at the Mayor, but now he could not say anything or object or he would have tipped his hand to admit his own deception.

They voted on the last item and the Mayor stood.

"We are adjourned," he said, banging the gavel and exiting the chambers into the anteroom.

The audience on the ground floor and the upper gallery erupted. Shouts and catcalls were heard and fists were shaken at the Councilors, who were surprised at the abrupt end to the meeting and the anger of the crowd. There was conversation among them, questioning what had taken place to anger so many people and what the message of the banners referred to. Not wanting to poke a stick at a hornet's nest, they swiftly left the Chamber, with only Carmichael staring at the angry mob but without enough courage to address them. He, too, quickly left the Chambers to hoots of derision.

The Mayor was waiting in the anteroom with a sly smile on his face.

"Don't you ever try anything like that again," he said to the miscreant. The other Councilors were baffled by the exchange but knew enough not to ask. They solemnly left the room under the watchful eye of the Mayor, as well as Henry and Bill, who had come downstairs to observe the final vote.

"I'd say this calls for a drink," the Mayor said to his staff with a smile.

Chapter 5

"What are you two girls up to tonight?" Mr. Burnside asked his daughters in the sitting room with one of the last blazes of the season in the fireplace. Cromwell, their Irish Setter, peacefully seated at Mrs. Burnside's feet, looked up at her periodically.

"Mother, what is going on with that dog? I think he's in love with you," Louisa said.

"I was keeping it as a surprise. Not his affection for me, but the fact that I signed up for dog training classes with some other people."

"What?" was the reaction from the others.

"I think he's very well-mannered already," Amanda said.

"Yes, he is. But from what the trainer said, he might be confused as to who his 'person' is."

The family stared at her.

"I'm his person when you are all at work and out of the house and, when your father comes home, he is the person. Mostly. I'm not sure how you two fit into the hierarchy of his affections or attention, but it could be confusing for the poor dog."

"So, you have decided to stage a coup d'état and make yourself his main person?" Mr. Burnside said with a smile.

"I am the person who takes him for a walk in the morning and I must say, I feel I have more energy during the day because of it. Although I don't know about the command of 'heel'

and he does tend to pull at the leash, which hurts my arm. And I want to learn whatever it is to tell Crom not to try to chase every squirrel in the neighborhood."

"Good luck with that," her husband said.

"Good for you, Mother. I've come to appreciate having him in the house, but I will cede my confusing 'person-hood' to you," Amanda said, making a gracious hand gesture. "If there is anything to give up as far as he's concerned."

"Fine with me," Louisa said. "And by the way, we're off to the Oasis tonight. There is some special singer who's come in and I want to hear her."

"Brendan and I will be in attendance, too. We're taking Louisa since Rob will be busy with all the hoopla. I think there were some posters in town about her visit so they expect a lot of people."

"How was your discussion with Brendan about the wedding plans?" Mr. Burnside asked.

"Interesting," Amanda said.

Her parents looked at each other.

"Are you planning some strange, exotic ceremony that we should know about?" her father asked.

"No. We didn't come to any conclusion about the nature of it."

"Not even a date?" her mother asked.

"Sadly, no."

"I'll bet there is the whole mixed marriage thing to deal with," Louisa said.

"As a matter of fact, obviously, that is the big thing," Amanda said.

Her parents were silent and she was forced to fill the void.

"As I understand it, his religion requires that I must agree that any children must be brought up in the Catholic faith although I wouldn't be required to convert."

Louisa piped up, "Simple: just don't have any children."

"Don't be facetious," her father said. "This is serious business although I imagine you don't have to sign a contract?"

"I don't know. I hadn't even thought of that. His older brother is a priest, as you know, so the family is very invested in their faith. We go to church on Sunday but if I were to measure it, our commitment to our faith in terms of time is rather less. If you look at it more closely, it really is an old-fashioned class-conscious prejudice in this country and a ridiculous five-hundred-year-old issue from Great Britain."

While her mother stared at her comment, her father applauded.

"Now that is a precious piece of critical thinking. That's why I said you would make an excellent lawyer. I may not agree with your final decision on the wedding business, but I appreciate that you recognize the origins of the matter. Good old Henry the Eighth was a very pious man and continued all the Catholic traditions, even forbidding the translation of the Bible into vernacular English. His only beef was trying to get out of his marriage and the Pope, his first wife's nephew didn't agree. So, when he made himself head of the Church of England, at first nothing much changed. Except he could divorce and marry whatshername. And then he went full bore, looting the monasteries for their land and money. Well, the rest is history, as they say."

"Thanks for the history lesson, Daddy. And diverting the conversation away from the meat of the matter," Louisa said.

"This is my problem to resolve, thank you," Amanda said to her sister. "I don't appreciate you stirring the pot."

Louisa got up suddenly. "I think I'll freshen up before dinner." She left the room quickly.

"Well done," Mr. Burnside said to Amanda.

"Daddy, stop making this all about your wish that your firstborn had been a son and lacking that, pushing me into the law."

That stopped the conversation for a few moments.

"Anyway, back to the original discussion, nothing has been resolved."

"Is a contract involved on his part or yours? What are the consequences for Brendan if you don't agree to bring the children up in his faith?" her father asked.

"Excellent question, Daddy. I'll have to ask him."

"I know that they are quick to refuse people the sacrament if they are divorced," he said.

"Really?" Mrs. Burnside commented.

"So, I understand. That's why they often resort to 'annulment' instead."

"Things are so complicated, aren't they?" Mrs. Burnside said with a sigh. "I'm sure you will think of something clever, Edward."

He looked doubtful but was rescued from further conversation by the announcement of dinner.

BRENDAN CAME by at eight o'clock, had a brief conversation with the Burnsides and waited for Amanda and Louisa to come down. He sensed some tension but maintained a level of conversation with the couple.

"There was this tremendous assembly of people at the Council meeting this afternoon," he said.

"What was that about?" Mr. Burnside asked, usually informed about local issues.

"I'm not quite sure. One of the officers who is assigned to the meetings came back and said every seat was taken and people held up banners. It seemed to do with children, he said, but of course he wasn't privy to what the items on the agenda were. He was there to make sure that there was no disturbance."

Mr. and Mrs. Burnside exchanged glances.

"How odd," Mr. Burnside said. "I follow the news closely and have heard nothing of great import before the Council."

Brendan shrugged. "Whatever those assembled thought would happen didn't. But when the meeting was over, there was an uproar from the audience, he said, with shouts demanding resignations or recall."

"Extraordinary!" Mr. Burnside said.

"I'll ask around tomorrow and see if I can get a better idea of what happened."

Just then, Amanda and Louisa came down the stairs into the sitting room in evening gowns covered by long dress coats. It was partially expediency to be fully clothed before leaving, along with Louisa's idea to keep her low-cut gown hidden from parental eyes.

"Have a good time and don't be too late."

"You can count on me," Brendan said, escorting the sisters out the door.

He pulled the car away from the curb and went several blocks before noticing that neither of the sisters had said a word.

"A bit chilly in here?" he asked with a smile. Neither of them answered. "Would you like the heater turned up?" he asked.

"No, I'm fine," Amanda answered.

The silence persisted until they got to the Oasis Club and stopped at the front door. One of the valets, dressed in what someone thought looked like Arabian dress clothes, came up to open the back door to let Louisa out. She exited without a word. He then opened the front passenger door to assist Amanda before getting the keys from Brendan to park the car.

"I hope we're not going to spend the evening in icy silence," he said to her. "Or if we need to have a separate table, that would be fine with me."

"If you haven't already noticed, my sister sometimes likes to provoke situations. And she was at it tonight."

Brendan furrowed his brow, knowing that it was an invitation to ask what they had been arguing about but thought better of it. Had there been something of note, she would certainly tell him as the evening wore on.

They were glad they had come early since judging by the full parking lot, the Oasis seemed to be packed with patrons who had come to hear the visiting jazz singer. As soon as they entered the club, they were met by Frank, Brendan's brother-in-law. He was dressed in a suit, his blond hair slicked down and his face red with excitement.

"There you are!" he greeted them. "Let me take your coats."

"I thought he was working as a bookkeeper, not a greeter," Amanda whispered to Brendan.

"I guess he's just helping out since it's busy."

Frank returned a few minutes later and handed them the coat check tickets.

"I was here when they were rehearsing this afternoon. They're terrific," he said.

"Come on. I've got a table. Bridie is here, too."

Brendan breathed a sigh of relief to know that Frank had brought his wife since he imagined the young man had been mesmerized by the glamor of the nightclub, the band and the singer.

"Where's Louisa?" Amanda asked.

"Up in the office with the boss," Frank said.

They moved through the crowded, smoky room past the potted palms, the room dimmed so that shadows were thrown against the murals of sand dunes on the walls. On one side of the raised stage was a piano with a man in tails playing softly; nearby was a small table where Brendan's sister sat wide-eyed at the scene. She smiled at their approach, relaxing her shoulders at the presence of familiar people.

"Gosh, I didn't know people would be so dressed up," Bridie said. She wore a long, puff- sleeved dress that would have been more suitable for a prom.

"These are people who go out all the time. I'm sure you don't with the baby at home," Amanda said. She felt a bit uncomfortable just then in her low-cut, sleeveless frock.

"No, you're right. In fact, I hope I can stay awake long enough for the performance."

"Don't worry, she's due to come on the stage soon. Mr. Worley was worried that too many people would try to crowd in here and it would alert the Fire Marshal."

"I wouldn't worry," Brendan said. "The Fire Marshal is probably in one of the private rooms there."

Frank and Bridie had drinks in front of them so he asked his brother-in-law, "What can I get you, Bren?"

The maître d', Vince, swooped in to ask the same question but was halted by the conversation.

"Don't go blowing your paycheck before you even have it in your pocket," Brendan said.

"It's kind of you, but we'd better go separate checks."

Frank leaned over and whispered, "Mr. Worley said our drinks were on the house. It's very generous of him and I don't plan to take advantage of the offer. Unless he offers it again."

"Separate checks for us, please, Vince."

"The usual?" he asked and Brendan nodded.

"Things seem to be going well. How do you like the work so far, Frank?" Brendan asked.

"Right up my alley. I was doing exactly that until the factory shut down. Your father offered me a job in either the construction or printing businesses, but my heart wasn't in it. I rather like working indoors with numbers."

"Construction is hard on the body. It's a young man's job. Look what it's done to my father's back," Brendan said.

Amanda looked alarmed. "What do you mean?"

"No one works construction who doesn't suffer some physical injury. For my father, it's his back. He wears a brace sometimes to ease the pain."

As they chatted, the room filled, Rob and Louisa came down the stairs from his office and moved toward the stage. Louisa's nose was no longer out of joint and she asked to join her sister's group while Rob went backstage to summon the singer. While they waited, a bass player came out with his instrument, another man seated himself behind a drum kit, another sat with a saxophone and yet another with a horn.

The piano player ceased and Rob came out from behind the stage to the microphone and stood there until the buzzing and chattering of the crowd became a hum. He was dazzling in his white evening jacket, a red carnation boutonniere in his lapel, his handsome face all smiles.

"Ladies and gentlemen. May I present the aptly named Melody Johnson." He gestured with his hand as a small woman with dark hair worn with a low side part and waves walked slowly to the microphone. Her deep brown skin was set off by the cream-colored, bias-cut dress that shimmered in the light.

The audience applauded as many of them were aware of her recordings.

"Thank you. How lovely to be here in Boston." More applause. She had a dazzling smile.

"But here at the Oasis," she extended one hand toward the desert-themed murals. "It's not cold—it's warm." More applause. "And I thought we could start out with something written by my good friend, Duke Ellington, who has allowed me to be the first to perform it. It's called 'Caravan'."

The audience applauded, knowing who the man was but being unfamiliar with the song.

As the applause died down, the slow percussive beat of the drums began evoking the vision of a caravan of camels plodding through the dunes while the singer began, "Night and stars above that shine so bright..." and the audience was in the palm of her hand.

As the drumbeat faded out at the end, the applause was deafening.

"Oh, wasn't that wonderful!" Bridie said.

After the clapping died down, the singer said, "And now, for something you probably know all too well." A familiar intro was played and she swung into 'The Sheik of Araby.'

Next came a jazzier number, 'It Don't Mean a Thing If It Ain't Got That Swing,' and she put her whole body into the song, allowing for each member of the band to have a solo.

They played for another half hour to the rapt audience, some of whom had not heard jazz played or sung before and, by the look on Rob's face, he knew this was a sure bet to fill the club, particularly on those weekday nights which were slower. The performers often had their weekends booked in advance and this could be a way to take advantage of the slack weekday nights. He looked over at Louisa and smiled at her. He knew that no matter how hard he tried, despite his economic success allowing him to be able to buy a house for his mother as well as one for himself, her parents still considered his business somewhat shady. But with the public engagement of Brendan and Amanda, he felt the ice had been broken and perhaps the notion of social class meant less after these times of economic stress for everyone. Perhaps he would move forward with the plans for their future.

Amanda looked over the crowd, which was standing room only toward the back, but even the people in the private rooms had come out to see the singer and the band.

"Isn't that the Mayor?" Amanda asked Brendan.

He looked to where she gestured and nodded. "As I said, there's the Fire Marshal. And the Chief, too," he said. "We're well protected in all respects."

"Nobody from the end room has come out, though," Amanda said.

Frank leaned over and whispered, "Those are the guys who don't want to be seen."

She looked at him puzzled.

"You know," he said.

She still didn't know but wasn't going to pursue it.

There were two more songs before the singer bowed and left the stage.

The applause was deafening and continued for a few minutes before she came out and took another bow.

"That was terrific!" Frank said loudly, to be heard above the claps and whistles.

"Do you think she'll do another set?" Bridie asked, hardly heard above the crowd noise.

"She very well might, but I think we need to get home," Frank said to her great disappointment. "Someone will be happy to take our seats, and your parents will be relieved that we're being responsible. Amanda thought Bridie was about to cry, but she mustered a brave face, gave a small wave and they made their way through the throng to the door.

"We can go in a bit, too," Brendan said. "Early day tomorrow."

Louisa appeared from the crowd. "I've got a headache."

"Can we take you home?" Brendan asked.

"Thank you, but I'll take a cab."

They stayed through the second set, which was just as electrifying as the first and seemed to have attracted even more people, making the room stuffy from the crush of the crowd. It was at that moment that Brendan nodded to Amanda and they got up. Several people pushed past with relief into the now-empty seats.

"They're a cute couple," Amanda said, thinking of Frank and Bridie as teenagers before realizing that they had been married two years and had a baby crawling around the house. It made her consider her position again and wonder what they would do about the families' religious differences.

"They are," Brendan said. "I just hope Frank doesn't get too enchanted by the allure of working at a nightclub."

"It's not as if he's on the floor mingling with the patrons," Amanda said.

"No, he's not. Sometimes he has a steady head on his shoulders but, as a younger fellow, he was always attracted to the fast crowd. My parents weren't too thrilled about them dating and then, well, the inevitable happened."

Amanda swiveled her head in his direction. "What do you mean?"

"Imogen."

"Ah." She had thought that might have been the case but had thought it indelicate to ask.

IT HAD BEEN a long and profitable evening for Rob. He was in his office ringing up the receipts on his noisy adding machine before putting the money into the safe, intermittently looking down through the window that gave him full view of the club. The waiters had already picked up the last of the glasses and taken them to the kitchen for a wash the next day. It appeared there was nobody else below, but he went down for his usual check.

Only Vince was still there, loosening his tie after the long night.

"If we keep getting crowds like that, we won't have to heat the place," he commented.

"It did get pretty hot, but so were the band and the singer."

"Front door locked?"

"Yes, boss. I let the boys out a while ago."

"Can you check the rooms backstage and the restrooms for any patrons? I've got to finish upstairs."

"Sure," Vince said.

Rob took some time looking at the receipts versus the cash again and wondered why there was a discrepancy. Were there so many comps? He would have to be stricter with the staff. It was one thing to give the Mayor and the big shots a free drink, but this didn't extend to friends of the waiters or customers from whom the waiters then expected a big tip at the end of the evening.

After about ten more minutes, Rob went back down the stairs and saw Vince near the coat check station with his overcoat on and gloves in his hand.

"Hey, sit a minute. We had a great evening, but what do you think we could do to make it better?" Rob asked.

"I could take a load off," he responded, removing his gloves, taking a cigarette out from the pack in his pocket and lighting up. He blew a plume of smoke up toward the ceiling, almost invisible in the dim light and the accumulated haze from all the smokers earlier. "The only thing I can think of is a bigger space or smaller tables."

"And a steady stream of entertainment. They were expensive, but we more that made the investment back. Are you working tomorrow night?" Rob asked.

"Al is on rotation. That's why I'm not hurrying home. Just finish this fag and I'll be on my way."

"Great night tonight."

"Yeah."

"Do you think we had enough wait staff?"

"They're young and fast, but if the business keeps up like this, we need to get more men."

"Let's close shop," Rob said, clapping Vince on the shoulder who picked up his hat that was on hatcheck counter. He put on his gloves, unlocked the deadbolt and walked out, as Rob made his way back upstairs.

A few minutes later, there was a crash at the front door and Vince stumbled in, out of breath and looking around frantically.

Seeing Vince from his window up above, Rob raced down the stairs to face the man.

"Jeez, you're not going to believe this. Somebody shot the Mayor."

Chapter 6

Brendan had been in a deep sleep when his telephone rang, and he leaned over to pick up the receiver.

"What?" he said after hearing Rob's voice telling him the news. "Call the main station. I'm sure you know the number. But I'll be there as soon as I get dressed."

Brendan was filled with dread at the implications of the Mayor's being killed. The terror and unease of the population thinking that someone of that caliber could be gunned down, the Chief now on the spot for what would surely be described as a crime wave, the implications for Rob's club and his relationship with Louisa. As he buttoned his shirt, he went to the kitchen and grabbed a heel of bread and stuffed it in his mouth. Looking around, he found an apple that would have to do to sustain him through what would be a long night. Fully dressed, with overcoat, hat and gloves, he went out into the cold night to start his car.

All the lights were on at the Oasis and several police cars in its parking lot had turned their headlights on to illuminate the scene in the parking lot. Rob stood outside, an overcoat and scarf covering his white evening jacket.

"Rob," Brendan said by way of greeting.

Rob raised his eyebrows with a defeated look.

"Did you hear anything?"

"Nothing at all."

Brendan wondered if he was being disingenuous.

"Did you hear or see a car leaving?" Brendan directed this question at Rob and Vince, who stood nearby.

"I came out and there was nobody here. Just Rob's car, mine and one other in the parking lot. The Mayor's. He was kind of slumped in the front seat and I thought maybe he had had too much to drink. Until I went up to the windshield and saw the broken glass and knew that wasn't the case. Helluva thing," Vince added.

Dominic Barone, one of the detectives, pulled up in his car and trotted over to Brendan.

"This'll be front page news." He hooked his thumb back at Gleason, one of the **Boston Globe**'s reporters who specialized in local politics. "Look who's here. He'll have fodder for weeks on this."

"How the heck did he get the news so fast? And a photographer with him?" Brendan asked, trotting over to the car to interrupt the photos being taken and irritated at the spent flashbulbs littering the ground that constituted a crime scene.

"Hey, Gleason. Have a little respect," Brendan said, but

the damage was done and the photographer was racing back to his car before he could be stopped.

"Do you want to comment?" Gleason asked Brendan, who raised his hand as if to swat the reporter away. Instead, Gleason smirked and joined the photographer and they sped off to make a late deadline.

"I'm assuming nobody saw anything?" Dominic asked. "Gleason probably got tipped off by the request for an ambulance."

"There's nobody out and about at this hour of the night," Vince said. "The waiters were long gone and it was just me and the boss, chatting after a long and busy night. Well, you were here, you saw what it was like."

An ambulance drove up, lights flashing, and Dominic went over to the vehicle.

"Can I ask you a few questions?" Brendan asked, taking Rob aside. "Off the record. Do you know of any hoodlums who were after the Mayor?"

"That's nothing I would know about. He came here often, but I understand he made the rounds of the better clubs in town. He didn't meet with any mobsters here, I can swear to it."

Brendan smiled. "Because you know who they are."

"Of course. They have their own private room and don't want to mingle with the public."

"Are you paying protection to any of them?"

"In a sense," Rob said with a crooked smile. "It's business."

"I won't ask you for names."

"And I won't be giving you any."

Brendan rubbed his chin, feeling the stubble coming in already. "We'll have to consider the parking lot a crime scene. I don't know if they'll close you down until the investigation is over or what."

"Who's they?"

"It's in the Chief's hands. He and the Mayor were close and I'm sure he's going to throw everything at it."

Rob sighed. "The Chief was here with him last night. Was everything okay with them?"

"We can ask his guy, Henry, although he left early," Brendan said. "Or the Fire Marshal." Brendan knew where Henry's loyalties lay but knew nothing about the Fire Marshal.

"I'd like to get a couple of guys in tomorrow to clean the place up properly if we're to be shut for a bit." He was also thinking of the stash in the safe upstairs.

"That's reasonable," Brendan said.

They looked over at the ambulance.

"Where's the Medical Examiner?" Rob asked.

"It's only a doctor. The M.E. doesn't do late-night calls. This fellow will make sure the Mayor is truly deceased, something Vince probably didn't do."

"He has been around the block. He knows a dead body when he sees one."

"I don't doubt it."

They watched as the doctor examined the body and the ambulance attendants stood by, shifting from foot to foot, anxious to get on with things.

Dominic came over to Brendan and said he would call for a tow truck to impound the car. "Where shall I have them take it? It can't sit in their yard."

"There's that large storage room in the basement at the station. It could go in there until Clyde and the techs take a look at it."

"It's a real mess, if you know what I mean." He grimaced. "Mr. Worley, may I use your phone to call the towing guys?"

"Sure thing. Vince, can you put some coffee on and see if there is something to give everyone to eat?"

He nodded and went back inside the club, Rob and Dominic following. While Vince made for the kitchen, the other two men climbed the stairs to the office. Dominic refrained from whistling at the tasteful opulence and the large window that overlooked the club below.

"Smells nice in here," Dominic said.

"Louisa was up here earlier before she went home. I like that perfume, too."

Dominic went to the desk and, standing, dialed the number he knew by heart. At the same time, he saw out of the corner of his eye that Rob was kneeling in front of a safe and was taking something out and putting it into a bag. The safe door obscured Dominic's view of how much money was going in the bag, but judging by the multiple motions in and out, it must have been significant.

After letting the phone ring almost ten times, someone on the other end at the towing company picked up.

"Sheesh, you must have been off in dreamland," Dominic said to whomever answered.

"I was out in the yard. Someone was trying to break in. Who is this and what do you want at this hour?"

"Your humble servant, Dominic Barone, Boston Police, requesting a tow job from the Oasis Club to the downtown station."

"Humble, ha! What, did somebody forget to put money in the parking meter?"

"No, somebody got shot and we need the car for evidence."

That stopped the wisecracking. "I can be there in about twenty minutes."

Dominic hung up the phone and saw that Rob was ready to leave.

"I imagine Brendan will want to take me down to the station."

"Sure."

"Fine. I'm not going anywhere. Let's go down and get a cup of coffee at least." He took the bag with him. "Wait a moment," he added when they were halfway down. "I forgot the deposit slip." Rob went back up the stairs and a minute later came back with the paper in his hand.

The ambulance attendants had left and it was just the four men standing in the kitchen, silently drinking coffee and eating slices of cake. When they were done, Vince put the plates, cups and saucers in one of the large sinks.

"Now what?" he asked.

Dominic looked at the bag that Rob had put on a stool and wondered what he was going to do with it.

"We'll all go down to the station and we'll take statements. You can take your own vehicles. You're not under arrest or anything," Brendan clarified.

The detectives went out first with Rob being the last one out, turning off the lights and locking the door.

Dominic said to Brendan, "I'm going to stall a bit and follow Worley. That bag he's got is stuffed with cash—I can't imagine how much. I want to see that he's really going to put it in the night deposit as he suggested. He sure isn't going to lock it in the trunk of his car."

"You think he's going to drop it somewhere?"

Dominic shrugged.

Three cars pulled out of the parking lot, but Dominic took his time starting his to follow Rob at a distance. He realized it was ridiculously obvious since the only traffic at that pre-dawn hour consisted of trucks. As they neared downtown, Rob pulled over in front of the bank, got out, looking around briefly before going to the night depository, opened it quickly and dropped the bag in. Then he got back into his car and continued to the station.

Only the few night staff were present at the station when all four men came in the door and the sergeant at the desk hid his surprise at seeing two detectives and two well-dressed men come in.

They proceeded to the hallway and, to prevent any accusation of favoritism, Brendan asked Dominic to take Rob while he interviewed Vince.

Brendan and Vince took their coats off and sat heavily in the two chairs.

"Do you need any water?" Brendan asked.

"No, just some sleep."

"Me, too." He pulled his small notebook from his pocket and a pencil and asked for Vince's full name and position at the Oasis before asking the man to detail the activities of the evening.

Vince chuckled. "The *whole* night? Come on! We were busy from the time we opened the doors, and I worked my feet off along with the waiters. There were so many people there that many were standing and the waiters had a hard time getting through the crowds to deliver the drinks and the food."

"I noticed."

"The only break we got was when the singer took the stage. Her performance stopped everybody in their tracks."

"Yes, that was something. Tell me about the private rooms."

"The Mayor always likes to have his own space out of sight of the other customers. Not like he's going to be mobbed like a movie star or something. He just doesn't want to be bothered with folks coming up and complaining about garbage collection or something. There was a real nutjob who came in a while back to poke his finger in the Mayor's chest about the clubs staying open past hours."

"I imagine he didn't take kindly to that."

"Yeah, well, the guy wasn't a customer here, either. He just barged in with a stack of papers in his work clothes and an attitude. Henry escorted him out pretty quickly."

"Must be tough to be a public figure."

"He makes enough from his salary and who knows what else," Vince said.

"Do you know what else?"

"Me? Nah. Those big shots are all on the take, I figure."

"Any proof?"

Vince became wary. "No, just shooting off my mouth."

"Was there any specific waiter attending to that party last night?"

"Sure. Saul. When the boss gets everyone back in to clean up tomorrow, he'll show up. Everyone thinks that the waiters hear gossip, but for the most part, they are working their tails off, going back and forth to the bar and the kitchen getting food, hoping for a big tip. They don't have any interest in politics or who is working what deal."

"It's got to be an exhausting job," Brendan commented.

"I used to wait tables and I tell you, when you get home, your dogs are barking something awful. I used to sit on the floor and put my legs up against the wall just to reduce the swelling. Then somebody put me onto the right kind of shoes. Makes all the difference."

"Don't I know it," Brendan said, although it had been some time since he had walked a beat on the cement sidewalks in all weathers. "If you think of anything else, give me a call, okay? Otherwise, I'll be back at the Oasis tomorrow. Wait," Brendan laughed. "It is tomorrow!"

Chapter 7

The story of the Mayor's being shot made it into the morning papers. The editor had held up the presses to have it be the lead story, but he stopped short of using the photograph of the dead man slumped in the front seat. Instead, he reluctantly allowed a photo taken at an angle that showed only the hole in the windshield.

Mr. Burnside was about to sit down for breakfast and asked Simona if the paper had been delivered. She told him that she had looked out onto the front steps some time ago and it wasn't there.

"I'll check again," she said, after she poured his coffee.

She returned a few minutes later with a stricken look on her face.

Mr. Burnside glanced at the paper, read the headline and got up so quickly that he spilled his coffee. He raced through the sitting room and up the stairs to tell his wife the news.

Amanda heard her father's heavy footsteps and, still in her robe, stuck her head out her bedroom door. But he had already gone into his bedroom and slammed the door behind him. A moment later, she could hear her mother's voice in distress. She ran down the hall, knocked on the door and asked if everything was all right.

The door opened slowly to her father's scowling face.

"No, it is not. The Mayor was shot and killed last night," he said.

Amanda put her hand to her mouth. "That's impossible. I just saw him last night hale and hearty."

"Well, someone put an end to that. In the parking lot of the Oasis Club, no less."

The icy feeling of fear gripped her stomach. "Was anybody else hurt?"

"I didn't read that far. The paper is downstairs."

Amanda tightened the belt of her robe and swiftly made her way to the morning room, picked up the paper and read it standing up.

Simona came in from the kitchen. "Isn't it awful? Would you like some coffee, Miss?"

"I can't believe this. We just saw him last night."

She continued to read the brief article that mentioned the location being the Oasis Club and said that an investigation was forthcoming.

"I'd better tell Louisa," she said and made her way back upstairs. But her father had beat her to it and was standing at the end of her sister's bed, his hands on his hips and a ferocious look on his face. Louisa was sitting up with her mouth open.

"I told you no good would come of going to that place and seeing that man! To know that my daughter was in the place where the Mayor of the city was shot!"

Regaining her poise, Louisa said, "Amanda was there, too."

Thanks, Amanda thought, although her father already knew that.

"I don't care if the King of England was there! If you ever bothered to read the newspapers, you would know that crime has been increasing, mobsters are everywhere, taking over our city. Now, they're killing our public servants. That Worley man might look suave, but I always knew his quiet ways were just a cover up for what he knows and can't talk about! I absolutely forbid you from seeing him ever again!"

"Daddy!" Louisa wailed, bursting into tears.

He began to walk out of the room but turned. "You are to be escorted to work at Monsieur Josef's every day and picked up either by me or your sister. And you are not to set foot in that nightclub again. That's final." He stormed out.

Louisa let out a pathetic wail and stretched her arms out to Amanda, who had no time to react because her mother had come to the door.

"How could you?" Mrs. Burnside said, her hair askew and tears on her cheeks.

Mr. Burnside reappeared in the doorway. "And you are not

to talk to that man on the phone. Or by letter or telegram!" He left again.

Mrs. Burnside collapsed in the vanity chair and Amanda made a beeline for the door, went to her own room, got dressed quickly and went down to breakfast.

Her father was looking at the newspaper and shaking his head. "Incredible. To imagine one of my daughters is mixed up in this."

"Daddy, let's be calm for a moment. We don't know that Louisa is involved in this at all. She came home earlier than I. The article says he was killed in the early hours of the morning."

Her father glared at her before closing his eyes. "I don't mean to take this out on you. But this is the worst scandal that has ever touched this family."

In a moment of clarity, Amanda said, "Perhaps not."

Mr. Burnside paused and then laughed. "Of course not! Families do everything to cover up their scandals."

"Louisa's name is not mentioned. Nor is Rob's." To herself she thought, *not yet*.

"We have to do everything to keep those dreadful reporters away from us. Maybe they don't even know that Louisa has been seeing Worley."

"There you go, Daddy. Bring your logic to bear on this. We'll do our best to keep her in check until this blows over. I'll see if breakfast is ready." Amanda went into the kitchen and was met with the wide eyes of Cook, Simona and Mary.

"My father is really upset about crime in the city." She knew she hadn't fooled any of them since they must have heard her father's voice thundering earlier. Still, keeping up appearances, "I think we're ready for breakfast now," she said with a smile.

They ate in silence and Amanda wondered if anyone would pick up on the fact that Louisa had been seeing Rob. If the Oasis had to close because it was the scene of a crime, the barmen, cooks and waiters would be out of a job. In that case, one of the Oasis staff, eager for a little extra cash, could tip off the press. For that matter, she had been there, too. As well as Brendan.

She excused herself, went into her father's study and tried calling him at his apartment first. It rang about five times before his breathless response.

"What's going on?" Amanda said.

"I just stopped home to take a quick bath since I've been up since the early hours."

"Were you called out to the murder?"

"Yes. And I've got to get back to the station right away. All hell's broken loose."

"My parents are furious about it, and Louisa has gone to pieces."

"I'm sorry there is drama at your house. But I've got a lot of ground to cover today and the press is going to be up our noses looking for information, clues, anything."

"Sure. I'll try to call you later today."

"Thanks, love. I might not be able to come to the phone to chat."

"Good luck," she said.

Amanda felt unmoored. Should she go to work as usual? Would everyone be talking about it and put together her connection with the nightclub? Then she remembered her words to her father to bring logic to the situation. No, probably neither she nor Louisa nor Brendan would be implicated by association. The previous night had been a huge occasion with a full house. Why should the Burnside sisters be of any interest to the reading public? Wouldn't they want to know who was with the Mayor? And come to think of it, who was with him? The Fire Marshal, the ever-present Henry, but surely there were others in that private room. And why did he need to have a private room? One thing she knew about the Mayor was that he loved attention and recognition. Was something else going on in that room—some deal, some exchange of favors—that they needed to be private?

Chapter 8

Brendan hustled back to the station, disoriented by the lack of sleep. When he stopped at a red light, he surveyed his face to see that he hadn't missed any spots while shaving but still had a tiny piece of toilet paper stuck to a nick on his chin. He peeled it off with a wince. All he needed was a gallon of coffee to keep going and maybe somewhere he could grab an hour of sleep for what was certain to be a long day.

The station was a hive of activity, No sooner had he come in the front doors than someone told him of the all-staff meeting in thirty minutes. Ten steps further in, Gleason stood in his path, notebook at the ready.

"What can you tell me about the murder of the Mayor?" Gleason asked.

"Nothing. As you can see, I've just walked in the door."

"Was this a gang-related hit?" Gleason asked.

Brendan kept on walking.

"Vendetta of some kind? A political killing?"

Brendan passed through the door that led to the bullpen where neither Gleason nor any unescorted member of the public was allowed. He let out a sigh of relief to be out of the trajectory of the reporter, but now he was swarmed with the detectives demanding to know what was going on. He held up both hands as if in surrender.

"I understand the Chief has called a meeting in the next half hour. We'll know our marching orders at that time. Be alert." He took off his overcoat as he walked to his office where Dominic was waiting.

"What a night!" Dominic said.

"You're telling me."

"I thought you told me you were going to the club last night."

"And I did. There was this fantastic singer there and the place was packed. The Mayor was there, too."

"No kidding. Was he the last one to leave?" Dominic asked.

"I have no idea. We left when things were still hopping. We haven't established if he was the last to leave, but if not, you would think someone would have noticed him in the car. I should pop in and see what Clyde's folks have found. I'm sure the Medical Examiner hasn't got to it yet. And being such a high-profile individual, he will have to be extra thorough."

Dominic blew out his cheeks. "You think only the one shot?"

"That's what it looks like. And a big wad of cash in his pocket."

That stopped the conversation.

"A thousand dollars in large bills," Brendan said.

"I'll leave you to it."

Brendan put his overcoat and hat away and went to the crime lab where Clyde Owens had his shop. He was there in his lab coat, tinkering with something.

"Hey, boss," Clyde said. "We've got a bullet casing for you."

"Were you out at the site already?"

"Early birds. I suspect we got there shortly after you left."

"How did you find out?"

"I've asked whoever is on desk duty to call me—no matter what time of day or night—when a homicide occurs so we can scope out the scene before it is contaminated."

"Good thinking," Brendan said, impressed by the man's initiative.

"As you know, the lot is paved but not maintained very well so a lot of dirt is on it. It looks like a herd of elephants came through."

"Every patron who parked their own car and a slew of valets who retrieved cars for guests. Not to mention us, Gleason and the photographer."

"Photographer? Really? We need to see those photos. That could tell us a lot. All that we could find on the ground, aside from some lady's glove and compact that got dropped, was a shell casing. Only one, as far as we could see. From a Colt thirty-eight."

"Great. Just the most common handgun. Probably at the bottom of the Charles River by now." Brendan said.

"I don't imagine anybody saw anything or heard anything?"

"No one is saying anything yet."

"Did the ME let you know when he might be finished?"

"I called over there hours ago and he wasn't in yet."

"He hasn't started? He'd better get on it. This case is red hot."

"Any thoughts just yet?" Clyde asked.

"It looks like a gangland murder. One clean shot. But who knows?"

Clyde came a little closer to talk more quietly. "Was the Mayor involved with gangsters? Why was there a significant sum of money in one of his pockets? It certainly wasn't a robbery. Or was he on the right side of the law and they were angry with him? Do you think they put money in his pocket to make it look like he was on the take?"

Brendan shrugged. "Good questions. Off to the Chief's meeting. You'll want to be there, too," he said. "Wear your lab coat. It always impresses people."

The other men drifted into the meeting early to get catch up on each other's personal lives as much as to get the latest information. The chatter halted when they heard the Chief's approach and everyone sat up straight.

"As you were," he said as if they had come to attention. He

usually leaned against the podium when addressing the troops but on that morning, he stood ramrod still behind it.

"Gentlemen, we lost the life of one of Boston's greatest last night in a heinous assassination. The man who championed this department, supported us through thick and thin, is gone. I'd like to ask for a minute of silence as we pray for His Honor's soul."

The men dutifully bowed their heads and a few could be seen mumbling some prayer although very few had ever met the man in person. If the late Mayor had been such a strong supporter, nobody in the room save the Chief was aware of what those actions had been. And he was aware because he had been appointed by the man and was a frequent drinking partner.

The prayer pause over, many men crossed themselves and then put their attention back to the Chief's now angry face.

"I will not stand for this lawlessness. We are going to track down the perpetrators and see them in the electric chair. Keep your eyes and ears open, talk to all your folks on the street because someone knows something." He glanced around the room.

"Halloran, what does the ME say?"

"Hasn't got to it yet, sir."

"Owens, what does your lab have?"

"One shell casing. Thirty-eight caliber," Clyde said.

"And no witnesses?" the Chief said, shaking his head. "No matter what anyone thinks, the gangs are not exempt from investigation." He stepped down from the dais and left the room.

"That's a new line," Dominic said to Brendan back in his office. "Just to be clear, one of my cousins works for the Morellis."

Brendan raised his eyebrows.

"In one of the stores the family owns. It's on the up and up." Then he added, "The grocery store is, not the family."

"If we go hard on them, will your cousin be in danger? Do you want to step back from this one?"

"No. I think he's safe. He's not even twenty yet. Hard worker and he's never mentioned anything to me."

"He wouldn't be likely to, don't you think?"

Dominic shrugged. "Maybe they launder money, but he doesn't work in the back doing the accounts or anything. He stocks the shelves, works the register. If he sees anything, he says nothing."

"Just what the Morellis like."

THE CHIEF GOT BACK to his office to face his secretary's worried face.

"What?" he asked.

"The District Attorney would like to meet with you."

"Fine. I think I've got some time at eleven. Have him come over then."

He walked into his private office and heard her following him.

He turned. "What?"

"He wants you to go to his office."

"Oh, he's going to play that game, is he? Call him back and tell him I stubbed my big toe and walking is difficult."

She pressed her lips together to smother a smile. "Yes, sir."

The Chief had no sooner sat down than she tapped on the open door. "He says he sprained his ankle."

The Chief guffawed. "Tell him I'll meet him at Union Oyster House at noon and we can have a talk on neutral ground."

The restaurant was a well-known hangout for politicos, and the Chief chose it especially because District Attorney Heller couldn't make one of his loud tirades without looking ridiculous in front of the other patrons. The two men had a tense, long-standing relationship, starting with Heller publicly stating once at a Democratic party event that he thought the Chief of Police ought to be an elected position. Even though it got him a laugh, he well knew that the City's Charter clearly stipulated that it was an appointment at the pleasure of the Mayor. To counter that crack, the Chief was fond of criticizing Heller's campaigning techniques by claiming he thought he was running for the Sheriff of Dodge City. Being of the same political party, they ought to have been working together, but each one thought the other was stepping on his toes.

The Chief got there first and was seated, enjoying a Manhattan, when Heller paused at the door, surveying the diners and stopping at several tables to shake hands and say a few words before making his way to be seated.

"You're not up for election for at least another year," the Chief said.

"When you're elected by the people, you're always running," Heller responded.

"Looks like the ankle is better," the Chief said.

"And your toe?"

"That's why I'm sitting down."

Heller flagged down a waiter and ordered a Scotch and soda.

"Okay, let's cut the crap. What did you want to talk about?" the Chief asked.

"My sources tell me you've got next to nothing on the Mayor's killing. My other sources tell me gangs were involved."

"Which one?"

"Take your pick. But you can be sure that Worley is in with them."

"How so?"

"Doesn't he rent out private rooms at the Oasis?"

"Yes. So? I often book a private room when I need to discuss sensitive things."

"Were you in the same room with the folks in the other room?"

"With whom? What are you suggesting?" the Chief's face was becoming red.

"Hold on. I just want to know if you're there and they're there, if you talk to each other."

"Don't be an idiot. I wouldn't be caught dead talking to those guys."

Heller smiled at the turn of phrase. He held his hands up in appeasement. "Just asking. Have you arrested anyone yet?"

"Why?"

"I think you should arrest Worley. He's too slick for my taste and it would look good for us to be cleaning up the city by putting some of these clubs out of business." The waiter arrived with his drink and he took a big slug.

"I don't have anything on the man."

"Yet."

"I can't imagine what beef he had with the Mayor. He was a good, solid customer. And that place brings in a lot of sales tax revenue to the City."

"Be that as it may, forces on the Council are wanting to curtail the alcohol business."

"Come on, we fought that fight already with Prohibition, and all it did was give the gangs control over illegal distribution and sale. Not to mention people with stills in the basement cooking up rotgut. I'm not going down that road again." The Chief took a long gulp of his drink.

"I still think I'll get an indictment against Worley," Heller said. "His customers will go somewhere else and we won't be accused of ruining people's entertainment choices or cutting the municipal purse."

"We don't have enough evidence for me to arrest him or for you to get an indictment," the Chief said.

"Well, find some."

The Chief got up abruptly and left. Heller smiled broadly at the retreating figure, not because he thought he had won, but because he wanted everyone in the dining room to think he had.

Chapter 9

Amanda had gone to work that morning grateful to escape the drama at home. Why her sister thought she was the one to mitigate their parents' concern, she didn't know. She felt sorry for Louisa, knowing that by her association with Rob, she had already effectively cut off her chances of forming a relationship or marriage with any young man of their own social class. Times might be changing, but she also realized that her own engagement to Brendan, an Irish American detective, had put her in the same category.

It seemed every street corner had someone hawking a pile of newspapers with the shocking news of the Mayor's death, and the law office atmosphere was tense with the thought that gangs had got out of hand and the city was headed for anarchy or collapse. As lunch time approached, Amanda left the office for a quick bite at the cafeteria down the street. Walking in, she saw Nora, who had worked for the Burnsides as a maid before she got a job at City Hall.

"Isn't it terrible about the Mayor?" Nora said, gripping Amanda's arm.

"It's too shocking to consider," Amanda agreed. "Are you meeting anyone?"

"No, I've only got a half hour for lunch, so I popped in here. Let's get our trays; it looks like there are plenty of empty tables."

As they inched down the serving line, Amanda asked, "How's work?"

"I got moved to the Clerk's office."

"That sounds interesting. What do you do?"

"We prepare the materials for the Council meetings—we have twenty-one Councilors, so just think of the paperwork that passes through our hands. I should say our tired fingers as we type up those many copies of memoranda and ordinances. It's quite an operation."

"Things must be in a turmoil there today."

"I'll say." She looked at her wristwatch. "I'd better just get a sandwich." Nora paid the cashier at the end of the line and headed for a nearby vacant table. Amanda followed.

"Some silly girl asked if we could take the day off in remembrance, and the Clerk nearly bit off her head. They've called an emergency Council meeting for later this afternoon and we've got new materials to type up and distribute to the binders."

"Don't talk," Amanda said. "Take your time and eat. I'll tell you what else has been going on. Briefly, our household is running smoothly, we now have a beautiful Irish Setter that my mother has taken to walking. I'm doing most of the investigative work for my father's firm, which doesn't take up all my time. And then I've taken on private clients."

"That's exciting," Nora said. "And I see you're engaged. Congratulations."

"Yes, Brendan and I still need to work out a date and all the other arrangements."

"And Louisa?"

"We'd better not talk about that."

Nora's eyes widened and nodded her head. "Boyfriends can be complicated." She looked at her watch again. "I'd better get going. I ate too fast. It feels like my lunch hasn't landed in my stomach yet. But you ought to come observe the meeting tonight. It may be historic."

"Take care," Amanda said. She lingered over her lunch, not wanting to go back to the office, in part because she didn't want to engage in the Louisa situation with her father. Nonetheless, when she returned, she saw his door was open and he managed to give her a small smile.

"How are you?" she asked him.

"Coping. As parents do," he answered.

"I saw Nora at the cafeteria. We had—I should say, she had—a brief lunch. She works in the Clerk's office and there's an emergency meeting today."

"I should think so. The Councilors need to agree upon a Mayor."

"Oh, so that's how that's done."

"Since he's been in office a while, that's the process instead of a citywide election. You can bet the Councilors have been burning up the telephone wires, calling each other and cooking up likely candidates. It could be an interesting meeting to attend."

"They don't do this behind closed doors?" she asked.

"It's got to be a public process. But you can be sure by the time the meeting takes place, they'll have narrowed it down to a few or perhaps one candidate. He'll serve to the end of the late Mayor's term and then can run for his district or an at-large seat. But my money would be on that person having established enough of a following by then that he'll run for Mayor himself."

Amanda thought about the political repercussions of the death of Mayor O'Hara and wondered if it could be tied to one of the Councilors. With that in mind, she decided she would attend the Council meeting.

THAT MORNING HAD BEEN busy at the Oasis Club as Rob and Vince had called everyone who had worked the night before to come in for what the police were calling routine questioning. Dominic headed up the project and brought Herb, Bob, Hank and Lou in to help. They had already determined what specific questions the staff should be asked, including whether the Mayor had been a frequent visitor, if they had noticed any disagreement or argument the Mayor might have had, who his companions in the private room were, if they noticed any interactions with people from the other private room, what the Mayor had to eat or drink and, finally, what time he left and with whom.

"Keep to those questions unless someone pipes up with something interesting that we should follow up on. In that case, stop and get me to flesh it out a bit. We've got a lot of folks to get to, so let's make it snappy."

"What about the band members and the singer?"

Dominic groaned. "If they're still in town, we'll find out where and get to them before they go on to their next engagement." Privately, he thought it was a long shot to imagine that folks from out of town would have any interest in local Boston issues—if it was for a political reason that he was killed.

As they drove over to the Oasis Club, Herb asked, "Do we know it was a homicide? Maybe the man killed himself."

Dominic looked over at the detective. "Good question, but seeing as the gun was not found in the car, probably not."

"Someone could have come by, seen the man was dead and availed themselves of a weapon for future use."

"It's possible, but not likely. The shot was aimed right at the middle of his forehead. People who kill themselves don't usually do it that way."

"Sure. I forgot you got called out to the scene."

"Yeah, I've been up most of the night. If I fall asleep at the wheel, give me a good nudge."

"I'm hoping the club will offer us all coffee and refreshments," Herb said.

Dominic looked over at him. "If you think we're going to have cocktails and hors d'oeuvres, you've got another thing coming."

They faced a room full of bleary-eyed people when they got to the club. The allure of the desert scene and palm trees when the lights were dimmed looked quite different in the massive, fully lit room. Rob and Vince had only called up those who had worked the night before, but it didn't exclude the possibility of more information to be gotten from other staff who had served the Mayor on previous occasions.

For once, Rob looked less than pristinely groomed as he had not had a chance to go home and change his clothes and shave, so he was still in his white evening jacket while the staff were in their normal daytime attire.

There were parking valets, waiters, bartenders and cooks to interview, and it could take most of the day to get through them all. Rob stood in front of the group of about twenty people who sat at the round tables bare of their tablecloths to let them know why they were there.

"I'm sure if Vince or I spoke to you on the phone, you know this is about the Mayor's murder. Right here in our parking lot. It's a sad day for his family, the City and his friends. We'll set up the detectives in the private rooms and try to move through this thoroughly yet quickly. We'll have food and drink if we veer into the lunch hour. Thank you for your cooperation."

Herb smiled, knowing he was in for a catered lunch after his usual scanty doughnut and coffee breakfast, but quickly squelched his expression to a more serious one.

"Anyone have other commitments where they have to leave soon?" Dominic asked. Some of these men might have had day jobs for all he knew. Only one raised his hand.

"Got kids to look after. The wife has to go to work."

"Okay, let's take him first."

Dominic assigned the detectives to their rooms with a pitcher of water and glasses thoughtfully supplied by the kitchen, and they got to work. Many of the men had left shortly after closing time the night before, with just a few on clean-up duty, which consisted of putting the last of the plates and glasses in the kitchen and the tablecloths and napkins in the bin for the laundry service. The cook and his assistants had left earlier, leaving the dirty dishes, glasses and cutlery in the industrial-sized sinks to go through the commercial dishwasher the next day. One valet was left to get the vehicles for the last of the customers, and it was he that was of most interest to Dominic.

"How long have you been working here?" he asked.

"About eight months. I'm hoping one of the waiters is going to move on soon so I can go inside. It's brutal standing outside in the cold in that skimpy Arabian outfit just to run to a car and bring it around."

"Did you see the Mayor leave? I'm assuming you knew which man was the Mayor."

"Oh, sure. He was a regular. In fact, I didn't park the car for him last night, which was odd. He came up to the front entrance and gave me a smile and a nod, which meant that he had parked it himself. It's usually the couples out on a date that want the valet parking. It impresses the women and saves them the trouble of walking in the cold from the parking lot. I think their dates think that's swell and we get a tip when they leave. Maybe the Mayor was short of cash for a tip, I don't know."

"That hardly seems likely. So, did you see him leave?"

"No, the boss sent us all home after all the guests had left."

"And what did you do? Get on the 'T' in your turban?"

The young man laughed. "Nah. A bunch of us shared a ride together. Just put a sweater and peacoat over the outfit, plus hat and gloves, leaving the headgear here, and we were ready to get home. It was a busy and long night."

"Make a lot in tips?" Dominic asked.

"Yes, indeed. Saving it for college tuition. I don't plan on being a make-believe sheik forever."

"It seemed to work for Rudolph Valentino. Until it didn't. Did you see the Mayor leave?"

"Honestly, we are so busy at the end of the night and eager to go home that you don't notice anything. Except if someone wants to slip you an extra tip. We are efficient and cheerful at closing, just thinking of that pillow and blankets when we get back home."

The other servers and valets also had nothing of interest because it had been so busy and, aside from the customers, they were focused on the entertainment. After a while, Dominic got the impression that his men were dragging out the interviews in the hopes that they would still be needed by the time lunch would be served. They could hardly keep that from their minds as the cook and his assistants were crashing around in the kitchen, having left the doors open.

Dominic finally talked to Saul, the waiter who had been assigned to the private room where the Mayor and his friends were celebrating something.

"What was his mood?" Dominic asked.

"Happy. A lot of backslapping and jokes as if he had scored at the racetrack."

"Did you overhear what that was all about?"

Saul became wary. "The boss has always stressed that we may be seen but we should not overhear their conversations."

"Come on," Dominic said in a conspiratorial tone. "We're always told that, but we also hear a lot."

Saul squirmed a bit. "It was something about work that made him happy. He didn't say but there was a lot of chuckling. Like somebody got their comeuppance. That's all I took from it."

"Any names?"

"Not names exactly. A lot of descriptions."

"Such as?"

This brought a smile. "Son of a bitch. Idiot. Weasel. And so forth."

Dominic laughed. "That could describe any number of people."

"You're telling me. But I did think he maybe had a bit much to drink. He slowed down toward the end of the evening and it was when the place was almost empty that the Fire Marshal helped him out to the front door."

"Were they often here together?"

"Oh, sure. Great friends. The Police Chief was here, too. But he left much earlier in the evening. There were some other folks there that I'd never seen before. Quieter men."

"Did you catch any names?"

"No. Well, maybe a Bob or a George. But no last names and I hadn't seen any of them before. Henry was there. You know, the Mayor's guy."

"Did he stick around until the Mayor left?"

"No, he left earlier. He usually accompanies the Mayor when they come here, but Henry isn't much of a drinker. One beer and he's done. I guess it's because he often drives the Mayor around. Has to keep his wits about him."

"But he didn't drive him last night," Dominic said.

Saul shrugged. "I guess not if he left before him."

There was a pause in the questioning.

"Say, you don't think they're going to close us down, do you?"

"Who?"

"The ABC folks or the City. Or you guys."

"I don't know anything about that."

"I hope not. I sure need this job. Best one I've had in a long time."

Just then a gong sounded and Saul got to his feet with a smile and a wink. "Soup's on," he said and left the room.

Dominic, the staff and the detectives were treated to a buffet lunch of baked beans, macaroni and cheese and brown bread, a hearty meal for a cold day. It wasn't the kind of food that was served to the customers but familiar fare to working class people. Water and hot coffee were on the table and not a few of the staff gave their compliments to the chef loudly. It was met with a sardonic smile.

Dominic sat with his men apart from the others and asked if they had got anything useful from the morning's interviews.

"They sure like the boss, from what I can tell. He pays them well and there's not a one who is thinking of leaving. That says something," Hank said.

"Loyal," Dominic said.

Rob was circulating among his staff, looking clean shaven and in his day clothes.

"Doesn't that guy ever look tired?" Herb said.

"When you're naturally handsome, it doesn't matter," Hank said.

"Like you would know."

Rob came to the table where the detectives were seated.

"Everything okay here?" he asked.

"Keep it up and I may ask to moonlight," Hank said.

"We'd be glad to have you. You can help keep the riffraff out."

"No chance that you'd let riffraff in the door," Dominic said. "By the way, there was another private room last night. Who was there?"

Rob looked as if he was searching his memory. "I didn't take the reservation. But I'll ask."

"Who was the waiter assigned to that room?"

"Again, I'll ask Vince." He smiled. "I can't oversee everything," he said and moved over to check on his waitstaff.

"That's convenient," Herb muttered. The others looked at him. "The food's good, though."

Vince ambled over to the detectives' table and asked Dominic, "You wanted to talk to me?"

"Sure, but I didn't mean to interrupt your lunch."

"It's okay. If it's a simple question."

"Who worked the other private room last night?"

"Moe. He's over at that table."

At the mention of his name, a short man with a large nose looked up.

"Thanks. I'll wait until he's done." Dominic was finished and was itching to get going, since there were things he wanted to go over with Brendan. He noticed that those who had finished took their plates and glasses into the kitchen and he did the same. After all, the waiters weren't on the clock.

"You're Moe?" Dominic asked him as they passed.

"Yeah."

"Good, let's go into one of the rooms. I want to ask you a few things."

They went into the room Dominic had been using all morning. He noticed that the man's shoulders tensed up, but so would his if he were on the other side of the table.

"I understand that you worked the private room last night."

"That's right."

"What group was that?"

"The boss would know from the reservation."

"Did they ask for you?"

"Who said that?"

"Just asking."

"I always work that room. And those men generally ask for that room. That's all."

"Was it some of Morelli's folks?"

"Who?"

"All right. Don't play stupid."

After a moment's consideration, Moe said, "Maybe some of them were. I don't ask names."

Dominic was silent as he wrote in his small notebook and Moe leaned forward to see if he could read the scribbles.

"Okay. Here's the deal. I don't know any names, but I figured they're not a bunch of architects out on the town having a few laughs. They're pretty jolly and all they do is tell jokes about each other and poke fun at each other.

Nobody talks business in front of me in that room and I'm fine with that. I'm in and out as quickly as possible."

"Did you hear any of them talk about the Mayor? Or the Police Chief? Or some of the City Councilors?"

"Of course not. They have nicknames for everybody. They called me 'Meeny' sometimes."

"What?"

"You know, eeny, meeny, miny, moe?"

"Clever," Dominic said.

"The Mayor was in the room next door, and he would have been able to hear them if they talked about him."

"Maybe they waited until you left the room."

"So what? And I don't even know who the City Councilors are, anyhow. They would just come in, drink a lot, eat and complain that the food wasn't what they were used to and leave after a couple of hours."

"I didn't say anything about City Councilors."

Moe said nothing in return.

"Good tippers?"

"They were okay. Ask anyone." Moe wasn't going to let on how generous they were in case word got out and another waiter would poach his gig.

"Okay. If sometime you remember anything, be sure to call me." Dominic wrote his work number on a sheet torn out of his notebook and passed it across the table.

Moe nodded and left.

There was nobody else to interview from the night before except a full house of patrons, the singer and the band, none of whom was available or identifiable. Dominic went back out into the main room and saw that everyone associated with the club had gone except Vince and Rob.

"Thanks for the lunch. That was very generous of you," he said. "By the way, where are the band and the singer?"

"Long gone. They left last night on their way to Syracuse. Not an easy life performing until all hours and then getting in cars and driving for hours to the next place."

AT THAT SAME MOMENT, Brendan was seated in the back of the Chief's car while an officer drove them to the home of the Mayor's widow. He wasn't quite sure why he was asked to go unless he was expected to take notes while the Chief offered condolences. It was one part of the job he disliked the most: interviewing the family of the recently deceased.

The Mayor and his wife lived in a middle-class neighborhood that was considered a 'good' one, meaning nice lawns and no crime. Somehow Brendan had been expecting a grander house, and the Mayor may have been able to afford one but probably stayed where he had begun his political career so as not to snub his constituents or look as if he was making too much money from the job. As they pulled into the driveway, they could see a couple dressed in black coming down the front steps toward a car parked in front.

"She's going to have to deal with a whole parade of people

paying their respects. As it should be, I suppose," the Chief said.

The driver opened the door for the Chief while Brendan managed his own and they made their way across the lawn to the door. Barely touching the bell, the door was opened by a red-eyed woman whom the Chief recognized, and to whom he gave a hug.

"Sally, I'm so sorry. Where is Mrs. O'Hara?"

"Just in here," she said.

"This is Lieutenant Halloran."

"My condolences, ma'am," Brendan said as he removed his hat.

"Let me take your things," she said, and they handed over hats, gloves and overcoats.

"She's in the parlor," the woman added, leaving the foyer.

"That's her sister," the Chief said quietly. He led the way through a formal sitting room that looked as if it was seldom used and into a space that was more casually decorated. There on a floral sofa sat Mrs. O'Hara, a tiny woman whom Brendan knew from newspaper photos. She clutched a balled-up handkerchief and began to stand up before the Chief addressed her.

"Doris. I am so, so sorry," he said, embracing her as she began to cry.

A noise from the corner let Brendan know that she had not been alone in the room. Her son, Kenny, had been seated in the dark and stood to greet the Chief.

They shook hands stiffly before Kenny guided his mother back to the sofa and allowed the Chief and Brendan to seat themselves opposite a coffee table strewn with magazines and newspapers.

"What an awful thing," the Chief said. "I'm sorry to intrude on your grief at this time, but I was hoping you might be able to tell us the Mayor's state of mind last night."

Mrs. O'Hara took a deep breath. "You know he always liked to be out and about. He thrived on knowing what the public was thinking."

"He was a master at that," the Chief said.

"I couldn't keep up with him sometimes," she said with a small smile. "I loved the flower shows and meeting the dignitaries and the political dinners. But then he liked to go out in the evening to 'take the temperature of the town,' as he would say." While she reveled in the memory, Brendan noticed that Kenny was not enjoying the nostalgia of his late stepfather as he leaned forward and took a cigarette from the case on the table and searched in his pockets for a light. He pulled out a silver lighter, ignited it and took a long drag before blowing the smoke away from his mother.

"Thank goodness Kenny came over so quickly."

"You don't live here, son?" the Chief asked.

Kenny grimaced. "No. I've been on my own for some time."

Brendan remembered the young man from previous encounters and wondered what it was he did but said nothing.

"Where are you working now?" the Chief asked.

"Hudson's," he said. "Head of sales."

Brendan lowered his head to write the information in his notebook but also to mask his distaste for the privilege the young man had through the association of his stepfather, who likely got him the job. Theirs had been a rocky relationship due to innate personality differences and Kenny's frequent mishaps from which he expected—and achieved—rescue. Brendan wondered how long the young man's job would last now that the Mayor was gone.

"Were you with the Mayor last night?" the Chief asked. It was a well-crafted question, suggesting that, of course, he would be out with him without pointedly asking where he had been the previous night.

"I was at my place. Just down aways in Brookline. Long day at work and I put my feet up and listened to the fights on the radio."

Whether he had or not, he was correct that there was a high stakes fight broadcast the night before.

"Doris, I'm here to let you know that we are pulling out all the stops to get to the bottom of this terrible tragedy. Our entire force is on it and we will get justice for you."

She put the handkerchief up to her mouth and stifled a sob.

"Is there anything you can tell us about his state of mind?"

"He was fine. He was ebullient. He never told me the details of what was going on in the city, but if things weren't going well, I could tell. He was in a great mood and said he wanted to celebrate with the boys. That's what he called you. The boys."

"I was with him and he was in a good mood, but I don't know why. If you can think of anything he was worried about or threats he had received, please, pick up the telephone and tell me."

"I don't know anything."

"Kenny, I'm counting on you to support your mother through this awful time. Have you made the arrangements yet?"

Kenney gave a blank stare.

"The church, the funeral home and so on?"

"Not yet." He looked to see if his mother was paying attention. "The Medical Examiner called earlier. I'll take care of things."

"If you need help with anything, be sure to call my office and we'll get somebody on it."

The Chief stood. "Doris, I'm so sorry. Please don't get up. Kenny will show us out."

The three men stood and after another hug for Mrs. O'Hara by the Chief, they left the room and made their way to the foyer, where Sally stood with their outer garments.

"Thank you, dear. Let me just have a word with Kenny," the Chief said with a sad smile.

She walked back in the direction of the parlor and they put on their coats.

The Chief turned to Kenny, dropped the smile and poked his index finger in the young man's chest.

"Listen, boy-o. You are going to take good care of your mother. You're going to move back in, too."

"I have to. The old man was covering my rent and I can't with the salary Hudson's is paying me."

Brendan thought the Chief was going to slap Kenny in the face. Instead, he took a deep breath.

"Take care of the arrangements. Move back in. Take care of her. Get a new set of pals. And if I hear you had anything to do with this, I'll pull no punches."

Chapter 10

Back at the station, Dominic and Brendan only had a few minutes to debrief their various interviews before having their scheduled interviews with the Fire Marshal and Henry Rogers. The late Mayor's aide had arrived early and was anxious to get through the meeting because of the emergency Council meeting. Brendan agreed and asked Dominic to escort him to one of the interview rooms while he went to the restroom. His first thought was that Henry didn't look as upset as one might imagine, having served O'Hara since he was first elected. The second thought was that Henry was now out of a job unless the incoming person valued the knowledge and contacts he had made under the previous administration. That is, if the new man intended to go in the same direction. Brendan couldn't imagine working in an atmosphere as charged and varied as the Mayor's staff, knowing that at any given moment or after an election, your job was at stake.

Brendan entered the room and apologized, saying that he had been at Mrs. O'Hara's home with the Chief.

"Poor woman," Henry tutted. "He was her rock."

Dominic nodded sympathetically.

"Can you tell me if there were any threats against the Mayor's life?"

"He confided in me a great deal, but he never told me of a threat. Oh, people would say nasty things to him when they were angry about an issue, but that's politics." He carefully brushed his wavy hair back and adjusted his glasses.

"Were there any constituent issues that were a problem?"

"He tended to defer those issues to the Councilors of the districts."

"That was wise."

"Well, he didn't want to interfere with the local, local political situation. And he felt that if something occurred in a district, the Councilor needed to step up."

"But there are also at-large Councilors," Brendan said.

"Yes. They tend to get involved in the citywide issues, not what street ought to be paved or what neighborhood needs a park. It's a careful balance." He looked down at his wristwatch.

"Any personal issues that may have led to the terrible events of last night?"

"No!" Henry said a bit more forcefully than he had intended. "Home life was fine, no problems there."

"What about Kenny?"

"What about him?"

"Did the two of them get along?"

"The Mayor adored his wife," Henry said.

"That's not what I asked."

"She came with baggage. He decided to take it." He closed his eyes and shrugged in resignation.

"Do you think Kenny had a motive?"

"Him? No. He wouldn't have had the energy to concoct a plan like that. Besides, the Mayor thought it best all around if Kenny moved out, got his own place."

"And a job that was arranged for him?"

"Probably. Someplace where he couldn't do much damage."

"Did the Mayor and the missus get along?"

"Oh, yes. As I said, he adored her. She supported him in everything he did and gave him free rein if he wanted to spend some evenings out with his colleagues."

"No arguments? No problems there?"

"Not that I knew of. What are you getting at?"

"Just checking all the boxes," Brendan said.

"Look, I've really got to get going. If you have any further questions, you know where to find me." He stood up.

"In the new Mayor's office?"

Henry had no expression on his face when he added, "I hope you got what you wanted from this conversation." He abruptly left the room.

"You don't think he's already defected, do you?" Dominic asked.

"I think you can bet on it. Whoever is next in line—or whoever thinks he is next in line—has been talking to Henry. He's a hot commodity now. He's the only one who knows what was going on in the mind of the man, the deals that had been made and those that were in the making."

A knock on the door and Abe put his head in. "The Fire Marshal is here. Decked out like you can't believe," he said with a smirk.

A few minutes later, Abe escorted the man into the interview room with the same look on his face as he looked over the Fire Marshal's dress uniform, which was quite impressive. Ropes, badges and medals adorned his jacket, and his hat had a large insignia on it. After shaking hands with the detectives, he doffed his hat and put it on the table, smoothing his hair.

"I'd like to begin by saying that Mayor O'Hara was a dear friend of mine and I am here to help in any capacity to find out who was behind the heinous act."

"Thank you," Brendan said, not sure exactly how to address him. *Chief? Marshal?*

"You were at the Oasis nightclub last night."

"Yes," he answered solemnly.

"Was it a social occasion or business?"

The man looked puzzled. "Business? What kind of business could we possibly have with one another? My remit is to make sure of the safety of buildings and gatherings, but

I was not there in an official capacity. I was there as a lifelong friend of the Mayor. He had heard of a singer and a band and suggested I join him for a social evening. That's all."

"I was there, too," Brendan said.

"Really? A social occasion or business?"

Brendan smiled. "Merely social. We had also heard there would be spectacular entertainment."

"Oh, yes. I understand you have an association with Rob Worley, one of the proprietors," he said with a smile.

"Yes, we are acquainted."

"Aside from the disastrous end of the evening, it was a spectacular performance."

"When did you leave?"

"After the second set. Early mornings for me, usually."

"And the Mayor stayed on?"

"Yes."

"Who else was in the private room?"

The Fire Marshal hesitated. "It was a private room."

"And this is a homicide investigation."

"There was Henry Rogers, well, you know who he is. I saw him leave just now. Your boss, the Police Chief, was there and several constituents."

"Can you give us their names?"

"They were introduced by their first names only. I'm afraid I don't remember. Jovial men who chatted about this and that and then the performance began and we didn't talk."

"All pleasant? No arguments?"

"Heavens, no. As I said, I had to leave but I noticed the Mayor suddenly seemed to be getting tired. He said he had had a 'helluva day.' I didn't probe further to find out what that meant."

"You didn't suggest he call it a night?"

"You didn't tell Mayor O'Hara when it was time to stop anything he had begun. That would have been overstepping."

"Indeed," Brendan said. "So, he was there on his own at that time?"

"Not alone. There were the pals he had with him and there were still plenty of people in the club."

Brendan paused to think that the Mayor had been left vulnerable and, if he had drunk too much, it would have been hazardous to let him drive himself home.

"Didn't you think you could have offered him a ride?"

"What do you think I am, a babysitter? If I had offered, he would have socked me in the nose."

"Did he tell you of anyone who had enough of a beef with him to kill him?"

"Look, plenty of people had some problem with him. Mainly because they wanted something that he couldn't give them. And he was immune to bribes."

Brendan's eyebrows went up. "As far as you know."

"I'm sure of it. He couldn't afford to be on the take. The hoity-toity folks in this town would do anything to take him down. And you know why." He paused for effect. "Because his name was O'Hara. Those folks wanted some stiff from an old family. But that's not Boston anymore. Those folks may think they own everything but they don't run much anymore. They're so afraid of the Irish they don't even know that the Italians are taking over."

"Morelli's folks?"

"I don't know anything about them. I mean just in terms of numbers. They're the new Boston. Now, I have some business to attend to back at my shop." He stood up, picked up the hat from the table and put it on his head and held out his hand. "Lieutenant Halloran."

Brendan stood and shook the Fire Marshal's hand. "Chief Reilly."

"I'll find my way out," the man said.

Brendan returned to his office, no closer to figuring out what happened when Clyde knocked on his open door.

"The Medical Examiner has been trying to call you," he said.

Brendan saw three slips of paper on his desk with the message that the ME had phoned.

He sat down and picked up the receiver and began to dial.

"No need. I can fill you in."

The receiver was replaced and Brendan gestured for Clyde to sit down.

"Obviously it was the shot that killed him but someone had already slipped him a Mickey, as they say."

"What? What was it?"

"Chemically…" Clyde began, but Brendan cut him off.

"Never mind that. Can you tell when that was?"

"The doc says that it was perhaps an hour before he died. There was that and alcohol in his stomach but not much in the way of food."

"That's a recipe for being unsteady at best," Brendan said. "Henry Rogers said that he thought the Mayor seemed a bit tired or out of it, but nobody made a move to take him home."

"Why?"

"He was celebrating a big win of some kind and, apparently, one didn't dare to suggest that it was time to go unless he said it was."

"And then it was time to go."

"I don't understand, if he was out of it, how he managed to find his way to the car in the first place. Why didn't anyone notice?"

Clyde shrugged his shoulders. "I think plenty of people stagger out to their cars after a night at a club. It's a wonder more people aren't killed that way. You could say it was a blessing that he was probably unaware of his assailant."

"Getting murdered under any circumstances is hardly a blessing."

Chapter 11

The Council meeting was set to start at four o'clock so Amanda made sure to be there half an hour early. Even with that lead time, the chamber was filling up quickly. She saw Henry Rogers scanning the crowd and he came up to her.

"Business or pleasure?" he asked with a crooked smile, remembering their first encounter in the North End.

"Perhaps both," she answered, a bit shocked at his ability to be jovial so soon after the death of his boss.

"It's hard to see from here. Come to the observation booth with me and you'll get a better view."

She tucked her notebook under her arm, put her handbag over her shoulder and followed him to the front of the auditorium and then out to a hallway, through a door, and up a few steps into a darkened room with a large window that faced the dais.

"Comfortable chairs, great view and the sound is piped in from the microphones on the dais. It's a great place to observe without being seen."

"Why does it matter if you're seen if you work here?" She sat down next to him.

"Sometimes I couldn't keep my face expressionless if I sat in the audience. And from here, I can signal the Mayor if something urgent has come up so he can call a brief recess to get updated."

"Do you expect all of the Councilors to be in attendance today?"

"It will be hard for some, since they had to take off work to be here yesterday. But it is the most important meeting in a long time."

"How long did you work for the Mayor?"

"Since he was first elected. I helped run his campaign."

The door opened and a small man with a bulging briefcase looked up as he entered the room. He didn't address either of them, just plopped the case on another chair and nodded.

"Bill, this is Miss Burnside," Henry said. "Bill Flagg."

He nodded again. "What's the skinny?"

"Carmichael has been working the phones since early this morning. So I heard," Henry said.

"Any dark horses?"

"Not that I know of," was the response.

Amanda had no idea what the conversation was about and, looking at Henry, saw that he was not going to explain.

"What's the procedure?" she asked.

Bill piped up. "Call to order, roll call. Carmichael, who is the City Council President, will preside. Only one item on the agenda. He'll open the floor for nominations, wait for a second, ask if there are any other nominations, and so forth. There are other methods of taking nominations and voting procedures, but our city has traditionally done it this way. Not that replacing a Mayor happens very often."

Amanda was wondering what would become of these two when a new Mayor was selected but thought better of asking it aloud. But it did seem odd that they were both so calm.

Bill clicked open the large bag that was his briefcase, rooted around in it and pulled out some papers, one of which he handed to Henry. The two men read in silence and Amanda looked over once, but it was just a list of numbers and names that meant nothing to her.

"I brought the afternoon newspaper, if you're interested," Bill said. "We're likely to be here for some time."

"Thank you," Amanda said, glad to have something to do while the adjacent chamber filled up with people. It was a long wait and she read about topics in which she had no interest just to fill the void. Finally, someone came out from a back room to the dais.

"City Clerk," Henry said.

"Oh," she commented, never having been to a meeting before and having no idea who the City officials were.

"He's got to be at every meeting."

Shortly thereafter, the long line of Councilors entered the room and took their seats while the crowd's murmuring became louder.

"That's Carmichael," Henry said, pointing to the man who took the central seat.

Amanda recognized him from photos in the newspaper although at times all these middle-aged men with their conservative suits and serious expressions looked the same.

He banged the gavel and the crowd was silenced. "Let's stand for the Pledge of Allegiance," he said.

The three in the observation room stood and murmured the Pledge as they heard the Councilors and the Clerk do the same. That done, they sat back down and Carmichael, as President of the Council, called the meeting to order.

"Roll call, please, Mister Clerk."

The Clerk read out the names of each Councilor in turn although several seats were empty. That done, Carmichael resumed.

"First, let us have a minute of silence or prayer for the late Mayor O'Hara." He bowed his head and the crowd was even more silent as the seconds ticked by until his head lifted and he said, "The order of business today is to receive nominations for the position of Mayor of Boston. We'll have open nominations."

One of the men raised his hand, indicating he wanted to speak, and leaned toward the microphone until he was recognized.

"Yes, Councilor Martin?"

"I would like to nominate Charles Carmichael for the position of Mayor."

There was applause from the audience and he banged his gavel. "Order, please."

The crowd was silenced.

"Doesn't he have to have a second?"

"Not necessary," Henry said.

Amanda noticed that most of the Councilors were sitting quietly except one, who looked around at his colleagues in disbelief. He raised his hand and leaned forward.

"Yes, Councilor Rouse?"

"I nominate William Rouse."

There was a titter in the audience and Amanda turned to Henry. "Can you nominate yourself?"

"Absolutely."

"Are there any other names to be put into nomination?" Carmichael asked. Nobody responded and he declared, "The nominations are now closed. We'll have an open vote.

"All in favor of Carmichael?"

There was a resounding 'Aye.'

"Roll call vote, please," the Clerk said and read off each name to hear 'Aye' again except for Councilor Rouse, who said 'Nay.' "The vote has concluded and we have Charles Carmichael as the new Mayor of Boston."

The room broke out in applause and the new Mayor

finally allowed himself to smile broadly and wave to the audience.

"That's that," Henry said, getting up.

"What happens to you?" Amanda asked.

"Bill and I will be working for Carmichael. He doesn't have much in the way of staff, right now sharing a secretary with three others. He needs people experienced in the issues the late Mayor was working on. There won't be much time for him to get his bearings."

"But he's been a Councilor already. And you said, President of the Council."

"Being Mayor is a totally different job. He'll be up to speed in no time."

Bill was packing up his briefcase but Amanda was looking at the spectacle in the chamber as the new Mayor banged the gavel and announced, "We are adjourned." The other Councilors gathered around him to shake his hand and a photographer approached with his bulky camera and took a picture, dropped the bulb on the ground to replace it with a new bulb and took another photo. As he fiddled with his camera, several other men stepped forward, likely from other newspapers, to do the same. Two reporters, small notebooks in hand, approached and began to ask the new Mayor questions although they were all far enough away from the microphones for anything to be heard.

"By the way, I understand you have some connections with the police."

Amanda blinked in surprise. "A bit," she said.

"Go on. What's the story with the investigation?"

"I'm sorry. I work as a private investigator. I'm not in the know about their investigation. After all, it was only last night."

"But don't they say that it's the first twenty-four hours that are important?"

"I guess," Amanda replied. "I have every confidence the police will do their best."

"They'd better. The Mayor appoints the Police Chief and if he thinks he's not doing the best job, he'll give him the sack. Let's go," Henry said to Bill and they started toward the door.

"Thank you for giving me the civics lesson," Amanda said although she felt she had witnessed a great deal more.

No sooner had she left the building and driven home than she called Brendan, hoping he was still in his office.

"How are you?" she asked, from the telephone in her father's study, still in her coat and hat.

"I'm so tired, I feel like my head belongs to somebody else."

"Have you been able to get any sleep?"

"I couldn't very well put my head on the desk like we did in first grade and take a nap. Things have been moving swiftly here." He told all that he could without compromising the investigation.

"I've just witnessed a Council meeting. And the selection of the new Mayor."

"Who is it?" Brendan asked without much enthusiasm.

"Charles Carmichael."

"Interesting. At least he's a law-and-order type of person. That could mean good things for our department. I don't know how he gets along with the Chief, however."

"Can the new Mayor appoint someone else?"

Brendan paused. "Probably. But I think it would be a mistake for him to make big changes so soon. I'll bet the Chief is already thinking of ways to butter him up."

"And Henry Rogers has already been promised a position with Mayor Carmichael."

"Interesting." Brendan's attention veered toward the hallway where he could hear someone coming.

"I suppose I ought to say goodbye now. You really need to get home and get a good night's sleep," Amanda said.

Dominic looked around the open door and, seeing Brendan was on the phone, pulled back until the conversation was over.

"Good idea. We'll be in touch tomorrow."

At the sound of the receiver being replaced in the cradle, Dominic swung into the room, holding a cloth bag aloft.

"You'll never guess," Dominic said with a smile.

"You're right. I'm operating on fifty percent brain power now. Fill me in."

Dominic approached and opened the neck of the bag. Inside was a gun.

"A thirty-eight, I imagine?" Brendan said touching the bag and not the contents.

"Yup. The garbagemen were dumping an ashcan a block from the Oasis and they heard a heavy clank and, lo and behold, a gun."

"Do you think it's *the* gun?"

"I'm thinking it is a definite possibility. We can have Clyde check, but I'm sure there won't be fingerprints on it. Even the garbagemen wear gloves."

"And if it is *the* gun, we can be sure so did the killer."

Chapter 12

Brendan did have a long, deep sleep and felt almost himself in the morning although he realized he had forgotten to eat dinner. No matter, he would stop by Joe's breakfast place around the corner from the station where he was sure to get a filling meal. On the way there he realized that he needed to interview the Chief about his night at the Oasis, just as he had everyone else who was in proximity to the late Mayor. If someone had spiked the man's drink, he wanted to know who the two constituents were in the room who might have done it and if anyone not expressly invited to the private party had stopped in to say a quick word.

Joe was at the grill with his sailor's hat rakishly perched to one side, his muscular and tattooed arms flipping pancakes and sausages. A young girl was waiting on the tables and, from her looks, Brendan thought she might be a family member.

As he sat down, she came forward with a coffee pot in hand and filled the cup at his place setting.

MURDER AT THE OASIS CLUB

"Are you Joe's daughter?" he asked.

She laughed. "No. I'm his granddaughter. I put in the breakfast shift before school."

"Good for you," Brendan said.

"Not really. Good for Gramps. That's why the whole family is trying to get him to retire. He works too hard."

"That's for sure. Two eggs over easy, bacon and toast. Thanks for the coffee."

"Sure thing," she said.

Joe turned as she put in the order and gave a wave with his metal spatula. "No time to talk this morning," he said. The place was full and Brendan nodded in appreciation as he drank his coffee and read the morning paper. Mayor Carmichael was the photo on page one. So much for the late Mayor O'Hara, whose name didn't appear until the obituary page that included the details of the wake, high mass and burial. It wasn't his favorite thing to do, but he knew he had to make an appearance at all of them to see who showed up and who didn't. Not that he had ever come away with significant knowledge. It looked like the late Mayor was going to be at the funeral home for only one day for people to pay their respects. Not the old-fashioned Irish wake at home with raucous stories, drinking and arguments. Fully American now, they blended the old multiday visitation with a modern funeral home.

Brendan peeked at the public notices section and saw that there was another Council meeting scheduled only two days after the funeral. Carmichael was moving fast. He remembered that Nora, who used to work for the Burnsides, had a job in City Hall and considered asking her to meet to find out what the new Mayor was like. It wasn't that important to the case at hand, but it might give him an inkling of the atmosphere there.

He devoured the meal in record time and was beginning to feel like his old self. After one last cup of coffee—a better brew than what he could get at the station—he paid the bill with a good tip for the girl and left.

Brendan was musing how to best approach the Chief about the night at the Oasis when the man himself appeared in his doorway.

Brendan stood but the tall, lanky man gestured for him to sit. He sat in the chair across from the desk.

"How are we doing?"

"Early days. We might have found the gun dumped in an ashcan nearby but probably no prints."

"Do gangsters dump their weapons like that? Isn't that a little careless?" the Chief asked.

"And we have to wonder why gangsters would be involved."

"Well, O'Hara was getting peeved about the level of violence in town and maybe somebody didn't like that."

"Politicians are always railing against crime. It doesn't mean that they can actually do anything about it. That's up to us," Brendan said.

"He was behind us all the way. If we needed more officers, he made sure it happened. He was a good man."

"Chief, I have to ask you, did he seem a little out of it that night?"

"What do you mean? He was happy about some victory that day, but otherwise the same man I've always known."

"The Medical Examiner found that someone had spiked his drink."

The Chief leaned forward. "He did seem a bit woozy toward the end of the evening, but I thought he'd had a long day and perhaps too much to drink."

"Someone mentioned that there were two other men there. Do you know who they were?"

"Tom, Dick or Harry. I don't remember their names. Ask Henry. One of his strong suits is remembering everyone's name."

"And there was Henry and you and who else?"

"That was it. Oh, yeah. The Fire Marshal, too. We were just having a good time waiting for the entertainment. That was something!"

"I was there, too," Brendan said. "I agree."

"Do you think it was one of the band members who spiked his drink?"

"I can't imagine what their motive could have been. From what I heard, this was their first time in Boston."

"Hmm. What about the waiters? They're sometimes a shifty bunch."

"I thought you always had the same waiter?" Brendan flipped through his notes. "Saul?"

"Yes, he's a good guy. I trust him implicitly."

"Nobody else came in the room?"

"It sounds like you are interrogating me, son," the Chief said.

"No, just trying to figure out how someone gets his drink spiked when he's among close friends before something even more terrible happens to him."

Brendan could feel the shift in atmosphere as the Chief glared at him. "He was a good friend to me and, if I had had an inkling about what was to happen, I would have moved heaven and earth to stop it. I'll regret to my dying day that I didn't notice the change in him as the evening wore on, but I'd had a long day and thought I left him in the company of friends. You've got to find out who those two other fellas were. They'll have the answer. And Henry Rogers has the key. He knows everyone the Mayor knew and he'll be able to tell you." The Chief stood up, nodded his head, indicating that was his conclusion and direction, and the conversation was over.

Brendan knew the Chief had probably not told him everything he knew, but now was not the time to push him. It might not get him closer to figuring out a motive, much less a suspect. All they had so far was the kind of gun anybody might have and a bullet casing. Why had somebody drugged the Mayor if not to incapacitate him to make shooting him easier? It had to be someone with a good knowledge of dosing narcotics; otherwise, the Mayor could have toppled over in the club in full view of his company and the patrons. That scenario would have been embarrassing but would not have led to setting the stage for an assassination. Somebody knew exactly what they were doing.

Brendan had a few minutes and called Amanda.

"How is Louisa holding up?" he asked her.

"Barely. She's decided to stay in her room when the rest of us are home."

"Is she on a hunger strike?"

"No, she scuttles down when Daddy and I are at work and my mother is out walking the dog. She's sworn Cook to secrecy."

"How do you know, then?"

"Cook can never keep a secret. She's always been fond of Louisa and is afraid she'll waste away. I wouldn't be surprised if Simona isn't smuggling meals up, too."

Brendan had to laugh at the family drama.

"It might be funny to you, but it has been awful here. Daddy forbade her from communicating to Rob in any fashion, but I'm sure she sneaks in a phone call whenever she can. You aren't going to arrest him or anything, are you?"

"We don't have any grounds for it. And what possible reason would he have for killing one of his best customers and ruining the reputation of his club to boot?" Brendan asked.

"True. I wonder if it will affect his business. Well, that thought for another day. There is something I needed to tell you."

"What is it?" he asked.

"Maybe you remember Cecile, one of my former debutante friends? She called me at home to tell me her father is on the City Council and that he and his colleagues are frightened about their safety."

"They haven't asked for additional security, although perhaps they ought to. Why don't you suggest that to her for her father's sake?"

"I'm meeting with him later today."

There was a pause.

"He wants me to help them look into the whole thing," Amanda said.

"Doesn't he know that their own police force is doing just that?"

"Don't take it the wrong way, Brendan. I explained that to him, but he sounded so nervous, I agreed that I could act as a liaison."

"That softens the blow. Somewhat. What do you imagine you'll do as a liaison? Pick my brain over dinner and tell him about it later?"

Amanda managed a laugh. "No. I'm not sure how it will work. Do you think this is all gang-related?" Amanda asked.

"If it is, you don't want to be anywhere near it. And that adorable dog, Cromwell, won't provide much protection. Unless being licked to death counts. I'll be by about seven tonight and then I'll pick *your* brains."

Brendan wondered why Mayor Carmichael hadn't asked for more security. Did that mean he knows he isn't a target? And why would that be? Brendan wouldn't share his concerns with Amanda just yet. He tucked it away in the back of his mind to pull out later to mull over.

Dominic came into view in the doorway, walked softly in and closed the door.

"What's up?"

"A little bird told me that the District Attorney is itching to blame somebody for the Mayor's killing."

"As he should."

"And that he is taking aim at our department and the Chief in particular for moving so slowly."

Brendan shook his head. "Slowly? Does he expect a miracle? He's just looking to make headlines for himself."

"I don't think it's common knowledge that the Chief was in the same room in the same nightclub as the Mayor shortly before his demise. The papers keep referring to the late Mayor's 'cronies,' not his friends," Dominic said.

"That's a cheap shot. No pun intended. Is everyone sucking up to Carmichael already?"

"Maybe he had them in his pocket all along." Dominic furrowed his brow. "You don't think this was a political assassination, do you?"

Brendan blew out his cheeks. "I certainly hope not. That could put the entire city on edge. Just imagining that gangs may be involved is a sobering thought. However, they are easy to blame because nobody dares to name the Morellis."

"Wasn't that who was in the private room next door to the Mayor's?"

"I'm not sure who was in that room. Perhaps Rob knows or Vince the maître d' identify them. Maybe they're scared to name names, too. What a mess. I'll call over and see if they can enlighten me."

"Before you call, I have the address of that guy Symington, you know, your friend who is always railing about late hours in the bars. He seems like someone with an axe to grind and he certainly thought nobody at City Hall was listening to him."

"Good point. Thanks, Dom. Let me know how it goes after you see him."

Brendan called the Oasis and was surprised that his brother-in-law, Frank, answered.

"Hey, how are things going?" Brendan asked.

"Everyone is very nervous. We're going to be open tonight, though."

"I suppose that's a vote of confidence from the District Attorney. Or the ABC Commission. Is Rob there?"

"No, he's out."

"How about Vince?"

"He's not due to come in for a while yet."

"I was calling to find out who booked the private room next to the Mayor's on that fateful night."

"Actually, I took the call. The name was Jones."

"Jones?"

"That's what he said. Robert Jones. Some kind of company meeting."

"Sure, that's sounds totally above board." He didn't know if Frank caught the sarcasm. "Thanks."

Chapter 13

Dominic went to the Newbury Street address that Mr. Symington had given when he last visited the police station. He had seen the man before and wondered what it was he did for a living that he was able to stop by the station and make his complaints in the middle of the day. Not to mention that he had late night hours, too, tracking which clubs were open, as he told Brendan during one conversation. The apartment block was modest but well-kept and he saw that the mail slot for the man's unit was labeled with his name. He made his way up to the third floor and rang the bell. No answer. He rang again.

A woman in a tatty fur coat leading a small dog on a leash was making her way down from the floor above. She nodded at Dominic.

"He's probably not in," she said.

Dominic removed his hat. "Do you know Mr. Symington well?"

"Only to say hello, although he doesn't return the greeting. He's out and about at all hours of the day and night."

"Do you think I could find him at his place of work?"

She stopped and stared. "If he works, he does it here. No regular hours as far as I can tell." Her look became wary and, rather than elaborate further, she continued down the stairwell.

Dominic scratched his head and decided to leave his card by slipping it under the door. Then he went back to the ground floor. He wasn't more than three steps out of the building when he saw Symington approaching quickly from the opposite direction that the woman had taken, his right arm tucked around a stack of papers.

"Excuse me. Mr. Symington?"

The man stopped short in surprise. "Yes," he said carefully.

"Hello. I'm Detective Dominic Barone from the Boston Police Department. I was wondering if I could have a few words with you."

"Not here on the street," the man replied and went into the lobby and stopped, looking around to see if anyone else was present. "Show me your identification," he said.

Dominic opened his overcoat to reveal the badge pinned onto his suit jacket. Symington peered at it, took a pencil from behind his ear and wrote the number on the top sheet of paper in the stack he held.

"Spell your name, please," he asked.

Dominic sighed and did so, wondering how long this interrogation would last.

"Did you want to talk here?" he asked, just to needle the man.

"Of course not." Symington looked around and went up the stairs quickly, as if not wanting to be observed, and Dominic followed. The man unlocked the door to the apartment and after they were both inside, he deadbolted the door and slid the knob with its chain in the latch in the device above.

"Just a minute," Symington said, turning to the living room and flicking on the overhead light switch.

It was then that Dominic could see that heavy curtains had been closed although it was daylight outside. The room was surrounded by bookshelves, some of them filled with tomes from floor to ceiling and others with tools and metal devices.

"May I ask what you do?" Dominic asked.

"I'm an inventor."

"That sounds interesting. Would I recognize anything you have invented?"

"No," he answered abruptly and put the stack of papers on a large desk next to several other piles. He then pulled two ladder-back chairs from the wall toward the center of the room and placed them facing each other. "We can talk here."

It felt like an official interview room with the bright, bare bulb illuminating the room from above and the two men eye to eye. Dominic pulled out his notebook and a pencil and, glancing briefly around the room, saw no couch or armchairs. The only furniture was the desk, a rolling chair, a gooseneck lamp and the chairs in which they sat. This was unlike other in-home interviews where the subjects would offer coffee or a drink. Not here. This man was all business.

"You've been to the station to talk about late-night hours of clubs in the city."

"After hours. That's right."

"May I ask where you were two nights ago?"

"The night the Mayor was shot?" he asked.

"As a matter of fact, yes. That night."

"I usually choose to stay home."

"Did you that night?"

"I had attended a very disappointing Council meeting in the afternoon that was supposed to address the issue of late-night hours through the adoption of an ordinance. But somehow that item was not on the agenda."

"Yes, I heard about that. What was your reaction?"

"Deep disappointment, since several Councilors had indicated that they were in support of such a change. Somehow Mayor O'Hara managed to get it taken off the agenda. In keeping with his devious personality."

"Did you know for certain it was he who took it off the agenda?"

"No, but it had to have been him. He was the only one with the authority to do so."

Dominic wrote that down.

"There were a lot of people at that meeting who went away disappointed."

"And you were one of them."

"I see where you're going with this, but although I was angry about the turnaround, I was not surprised."

"Were you at home or not that night? Did anyone see you or talk to you?"

"I don't talk to anyone in this building. They're a bunch of busybodies who act like I'm an alchemist who is either going to discover how to turn base metals into gold or blow up the building trying. If they don't fix the steam heat soon, I just might try the latter. My neighbors don't interest me. I use the mail to communicate with my scientific colleagues. I don't even have a telephone."

"You still haven't answered my question."

Symington was silent.

"We can do this down at the station."

"I don't have to tell you where I was," he replied.

Dominic let out a sigh.

"Do you think one or more of the people at the meeting might have wished harm on the Mayor?"

"I imagine a great number of them did. But they seemed to be rational people by and large and know that his death doesn't mean the problem will go away. I am merely speculating because, even though we share a similar goal, I don't know any of them personally."

"Okay, one last time. Were you here all night or not?"

"Even if I said I was, there is nobody to corroborate it."

"I think we're done here," Dominic said, snapping his small notebook closed. He stood and pointed at the obstinate man. "But don't think we're done with you."

AFTER LUNCH, the Chief had just settled down to signing correspondence that had piled up when a letter was hand-delivered from the office of the District Attorney. Opening it, he found that Heller requested his presence for an interview in the matter of the death of Mayor O'Hara.

The Chief slammed the paper down on the desktop and issued a string of profanities directed at the man.

Then, he shouted for his long-time secretary. "Mrs. Russell!" She appeared at the door. His face was almost scarlet and she was afraid he might keel over.

He sputtered. "You tell that…you tell him that I'll be over directly!"

He was furious, but he would show Heller what he was made of. If they went head-to-head, he had a rougher background and years of experience dealing with these toffee-nosed lawyers. Heller wanted a villain, but he wasn't the one who would look ridiculous in the end.

The Chief put on his overcoat and stalked out of his office. No sooner had he reached the front door of the station than he encountered a bank of reporters and photographers. It took all his strength not to lash out at them or say anything to expose weakness.

"Good afternoon, gentlemen. What can I help you with?" he said smoothly.

That issued a torrent of questions about the O'Hara case: what did he know about who killed the late Mayor, how long had they been friends, was it true they were at a strip club the night the Mayor died, why did the District Attorney want to talk to him, why was there such an increase in crime in the city, and did he expect that the current Mayor was going to keep him in his position.

He plastered a smile on his face and ran the gauntlet, waving a bit as he did, and stepped into the waiting car with a sergeant who was assigned to be his driver.

"Step on it," he said. "And if you hit one of those guys, don't worry, I'll get you out of it."

The driver pressed his lips together to hide his laughter although he knew the Chief could very well be capable of what he said.

"We're going to the District Attorney's office, where I expect he thinks he's going to cook my goose."

Attracted by the flash of the cameras, all the detectives had swarmed to the windows overlooking the entrance to the building.

"What's that about?" Abe asked. "Looking for updates on the Mayor's case?"

"Probably," Bob said.

"What's going on?" Brendan asked, hearing there was some commotion outside.

"Just the Chief telling those guys what's what," someone said, resuming his seat.

"What's the word out on the street? Has anybody heard anything?"

Bob said, "As usual, nobody knows anything. But everybody wants to point to the gangs."

"An easy out," Herb said.

"Nothing specific, though?" Brendan asked.

"Nah."

"Okay, men."

NOT TOO FAR AWAY, Amanda was on her way to see her friend's father, Mr. Peabody, at his club.

He met her in the lobby and shook her hand warmly.

"I'm so glad there is someone I can talk to about this," he said in hushed tones. "Let's go into the sitting room where women are allowed. He led the way into a quiet room with thick carpets and full bookcases although there was nobody there to read them at that time in the afternoon. They sat in armchairs by a window, far from anyone else who might come in.

"Thank you for agreeing to talk to me." He rubbed his hands together as they sat down, clearly nervous about talking about the issue. "There has been some skullduggery going on in City Hall."

"Oh," was the only reply that Amanda could come up with.

A waiter appeared and she thought Mr. Peabody would jump out of his seat.

"May I get you anything?"

"Tea would be wonderful," Amanda said.

"Whiskey and soda," he said.

He paused until the waiter was out of sight, then leaned forward to continue.

"Now I'm not of one clique or the other, but there are clearly two factions at work on the Council. It's political but it has nothing to do with political parties. One group follows Carmichael and the other the Mayor. I should say, the late Mayor O'Hara. Although as to who is going to pick up the pieces, it might be Martin."

Amanda had seen these names in the newspaper but she just imagined they were functionaries doing a job to which they were elected, not men vying to grab the reins of power. And of what did that power exist? Notoriety? Fame? Or was money involved?

"And what is the new Mayor's aim?"

"He wants to cozy up to the folks who ambushed us at the last meeting. The family and faith folks. Not that I don't support family and faith, mind you. I'm no teetotaler, as you can guess, and I can sympathize with people being worried about bars and clubs being open until all hours. But these folks want to take us back to Prohibition. That didn't work. It just created gangs who controlled the illegal liquor business and speakeasies. We don't want to go back to that."

"I understand."

He leaned in further to whisper although there was nobody else in the room, "I heard that Carmichael sneaked some wording into another ordinance we were voting on—which had nothing to do with club hours—that would limit the hours that bars and clubs could be open. I don't know if the Clerk was in on it or not, but O'Hara got wind of it I heard he switched out the paperwork." He nodded to her as if that explained everything.

"And?" she asked.

"It was a blow to Carmichael and made him look bad in front of all those people his staff had urged to come to the meeting. That's why O'Hara was so smug and full of himself. He had tricked the weasel!" He smiled.

"Mr. Peabody, you wanted to talk to me about getting security for you and your fellow Councilmen, is that correct?"

"Yes, indeed. Since the mayor was gunned down, we're very worried about our own safety. Especially since nobody knows why or who did the deed. That leaves us all open to wondering what the perpetrator could have in mind."

"Surely there is security in City Hall? I've seen several men in uniform in the lobby and patrolling the perimeter."

"We may need something stronger."

"Can't you take it up with Mayor Carmichael? It would be in his best interest, too, I would think."

Mr. Peabody looked at her warily. "You'd think so. As long as he's not involved in this business, too."

Chapter 14

The Chief reached the District Attorney's building to face the same scrum of reporters and photographers from the police station waiting outside for him to appear. How they got there before he did, he couldn't imagine, and he was about to berate the driver but thought better of it. Once again, he emerged smiling but noncommunicative, with the men shouting questions at him. He knew that Heller had tipped them off and he was going to give that man a tongue-lashing when he got up to his office. As anxious as he was to get up there and launch into him, he feigned nonchalance and got in the elevator and chatted with the attendant.

Once at the appropriate floor, he took off his hat and walked slowly to Heller's outer office. And what an office it was—leather couch in the waiting room, a gorgeous young woman receptionist and a floral arrangement on a side table.

"May I get you something to drink? Coffee? Tea? Water?"

"No, thank you, dear. I'm sure Mr. Heller has something stronger for me. As long as it's not hemlock."

She smiled, evidently having no idea what that was, and resumed her seat.

The Chief seethed at the notion that Heller had someone to just sit in a reception room, answer the phone and serve refreshments when his department was understaffed. There wasn't even a typewriter in sight. He took off his coat and hat, knowing that Heller was going to make him wait longer in another petty power play, so he reached over to the table next to the couch and perused the selection of publications. Law journals. Just to remind anyone coming in that the man had indeed got a law degree. Uncharacteristically, Heller came out of his office shortly thereafter.

"Sorry to keep you waiting, Chief. Come in," and he made a wide, welcoming gesture with his arm.

"No booby traps?" the Chief asked, looking around.

Heller chuckled a little too heartily for the Chief's taste. Something was up. Heller sat behind his desk and steepled his fingers in front of his face and furrowed his brow.

"Things are heating up. I'm getting a lot of calls about rampant crime although I believe that is an exaggeration. People want us to find the person responsible."

"Of course. We all do."

"It will put people's mind at ease knowing that we've done something."

The Chief was wondering why Heller had switched to 'us' and 'we.'

"Are you sure that you didn't notice anything untoward at the club that night with the Mayor?"

"Look, I have already been interviewed by the head of my detective squad."

"Halloran?"

"Yes, he's very thorough."

"Don't you think you should have been interviewed by someone other than a man who reports to you?"

The Chief said nothing.

"Well, be that as it may," Heller said, slapping both hands on the desk and smiling. "I had a talk with Judge Poster about an hour ago and he has agreed to issue a warrant." He paused to see if the Chief would get red in the face as he usually did when trying to suppress anger.

"A warrant for the arrest of Rob Worley," Heller said.

"What? That's all you could come up with?"

"He was there. It's his club's parking lot."

"Don't be ridiculous. Worley has done his utmost to be above board in all his dealings. He likes to keep his nose clean,"

"Except during Prohibition."

"That was another time. What earthly reason would he have for killing the Mayor? A steady customer, I might add. And destroying the reputation of his club?"

"It's probably the end of his business," Heller said.

"So, you think that is a justifiable reason to have him arrested and tried?"

"Have you got any other suspects?"

The Chief stood. "It may take some time getting that warrant served," he said.

"I wouldn't worry. I talked to a…" he paused to look at a slip of paper… "Sergeant Duncan and told him it was a great matter of public safety. "It's probably already been done."

The Chief's face did turn red at that point, but he said nothing and stalked out of the room.

AMANDA GOT BACK to her office and thought she ought to tell Brendan about her conversation with Peabody. After all, she concluded, his concerns about his safety and that of his colleagues were warranted, and the police should know about it. Besides, she just wanted to hear his voice.

"Are you busy?" she asked when he picked up the phone.

"Busy? Me?"

She laughed. "I meant, are you in the middle of a meeting or interrogation? Do you have a moment to talk?" She crossed her legs and sat back in her desk chair.

"This is the calm before the storm, I'm afraid."

"What does that mean?"

"I missed seeing you today. And I'd love to have dinner with you, but I can't. I've got to work late, and I'm still missing a couple of hours of shut eye as it is."

"That's fine. I understand. I wanted to tell you that I met

with Council Member Peabody for a bit and he is very worried about the security at the Council Chambers."

"He should be. I think they have one off-duty policeman and that's it. That's not enough to handle a huge crowd if things get ugly."

"It was large, but these seemed to be orderly citizens who were there to promote a particular idea or protest one."

"Nonetheless, one of them could have been the person who shot the Mayor. We always think we can tell who is going to lose their temper and act out, but it is not as simple as that."

Amanda was silent for a few moments and a shiver went down her spine, thinking that she had been at that meeting.

"I do have some bad news for you, though. The District Attorney went ahead and got a judge to issue a warrant for Rob's arrest."

Amanda gasped. "What? Why? Just because he runs the place?"

"I don't know the reasoning behind it except that they need a scapegoat and who better than some good-looking man who operates a nightclub and must be rolling in dough? As you well know, everyone assumes that something else must be going on there."

"Is this public knowledge yet?"

"I don't know."

"Louisa will be beside herself. My father is still in his office so I'm assuming he hasn't heard the news."

"If Heller is up to his usual tricks, he'll have tipped off the newspapers and you'll see it soon enough."

"Oh, no. I'd better get home before all hell breaks loose. I've got to get going," Amanda said and hung up the phone. She grabbed her coat, hat and handbag and made a beeline for the elevator. At that very moment, her father came out into the reception area and saw her.

"What's the hurry?" he asked.

"I just forgot to do something. I'll see you at dinner, Daddy. Er—Mr. Burnside."

The elevator arrived and she managed a smile before the doors closed on her, but she could tell by the look on her father's face that he knew something was up. She raced to her car and left the parking lot as quickly as possible in the event her father had thought to follow her.

As she drove, all she could think was that this had to be the end of Louisa and Rob's relationship. If the public was looking for someone to blame, they would find it in the self-assured man who had come up from nothing, someone a jury would love to see locked up in prison. Louisa could never redeem their relationship, and her family would also suffer from this terrible disgrace. Her poor mother! She would be shunned by people she had known all her life and her social connections would dwindle. And what about herself? Now her engagement to an Irish American detective didn't seem so radical. She shook her head to get rid of that thought, which smacked of snobbery or gloating or both. She just had to get home before the world crumbled around them.

As she pulled up to the garage at the back of the house, she saw her mother coming down the alley with Cromwell placidly walking beside her. What a picture they made. Her mother bundled up against the late afternoon chill, roses in her cheeks and the Irish Setter's red coat rippling with each step. He recognized her car and when she got out, he stepped up the pace.

"Don't you look jolly," Amanda said, faking a light-hearted voice.

"You're home early," her mother said.

"I had a long day." She gave her mother a kiss on the cheek.

"You and your father. Work, work all the time. I hope when you're married that you won't want to work anymore."

"We'll see," Amanda responded.

They went into the house from the back stairs that led to the garage and Cromwell made a dash to his water bowl in the corner of the kitchen.

"Smells wonderful," Amanda said to Cook, who cocked her head sensing something was amiss.

"Shepherd's pie. A good hearty dish."

And a good use of the previous day's roast, mixed with gravy and topped with mashed potatoes.

"How's Louisa?" Amanda asked as she took off her gloves and coat.

"Still moping," her mother said.

"I'll just pop up and see her," Amanda said as casually as she could manage. She dreaded telling her sister about the newest events, but knew she had to be the one to do it.

Before heading to her sister's room, she went to their shared bathroom, ran the tap until the water got hot, all the while looking in the mirror. She splashed her face and tidied her hair before approaching Louisa's closed door. She knocked.

"Who is it?"

"Easter Bunny," Amanda responded and opened the door.

Louisa was propped in bed, dressed in pajamas and robe and reading a book.

"Haven't you even got dressed today?"

"What's the point? I'm in jail. They may as well give me striped pajamas."

"Don't be ridiculous. What has Monsieur Josef got to say about his favorite designer being holed up?"

"I told him I had the flu. That scared him enough that he didn't want me to come near. Oh, but here's some good news. Rob called José in Florida where he and Caroline have been visiting his parents, told him what had happened and José said he couldn't leave but would call some folks here to help."

"You talked to Rob?"

"Er—yes. It was a short call."

"You know Daddy was very specific that you are not to be in contact with him."

"That's so unreasonable! I'm sure Brendan and his men will get to the bottom of this and find out who the culprit is. It will all blow over."

Amanda was silent but sat at the end of the bed.

"What?" Louisa asked, finally looking up from her book.

"Bad news, I'm afraid. They've arrested Rob for the murder."

Louisa didn't move for a few moments but went very pale. "How do you know?"

"Brendan told me."

"So, your fiancé arrested mine?"

"Since when are you engaged?" Amanda asked.

"None of your business."

"This whole thing is our family's business. And Brendan didn't arrest him. The District Attorney got a judge to issue the warrant."

Louisa began to cry. "It's not possible!"

"It looks like someone wants to wrap this thing up as quickly as possible." Amanda got up to sit next to her sister and put her arm around her shoulders. "The police haven't come to any conclusions as far as I know. They'd like to think it is gang related."

"That's something to go on, isn't it?" Louisa asked.

"And very dangerous to approach. It seems nobody wants to stir up a hornet's nest."

"And an innocent man must suffer so nobody else is disturbed? That's not right! It's not fair!"

Amanda nodded in agreement.

"You've got to help him."

"What can I do?"

"What you always do. You figure things out. I know you can, especially working with Brendan."

Amanda turned to face her. "The man you just besmirched by suggesting he was behind the arrest?"

"Sorry," Louisa said, batting her eyes at her sister.

Amanda sighed. "I'll do what I can."

Louisa threw her arms around Amanda and hugged her.

There was a tremendous crash from downstairs and Amanda jumped up to see what it was. Heavy footsteps followed and she realized her father was home, had slammed the front door and was on his way up the stairs.

"Where is that girl?" he shouted.

Chapter 15

Brendan was at his desk drinking a cup of coffee in a vain attempt to fend off lethargy when the telephone rang.

"Hey, this is Joe."

"Hello," Brendan responded, surprised to receive a call from the man with whom he usually only interacted at the luncheonette.

"Someone wants to talk to you."

"Who?"

"Just come on over," he said and hung up.

"I'll be back in a bit," he said to Dominic, putting on his coat as he walked through the bullpen.

Joe's place was just down the street and around the corner and he got there quickly. The CLOSED sign was hanging inside; he tried the handle but it was locked. Joe appeared, opened the door a crack, looked around and ushered him in.

"Wait here," he said and went back to the booths, leaned over one and then came back.

"He wants you to sit in the booth behind him so you can't see his face."

Brendan raised his eyebrows. "Okay." He took off his hat and walked over to the place where he was to sit. He saw the edge of a man's brown shoe and could smell the cigarette odor from his clothes.

"Well?" Brendan began.

"Look, you didn't hear it from me," the man with a Southie accent said.

"I'm not hearing anything at the moment."

"It's best if you stop poking around."

"Thanks for the advice, but that's my job. Anyway, it's out of my hands since someone has been arrested."

"Yeah, I heard. Everyone wants someone to take the rap and get the heat off."

"Are you with the Morellis?" Brendan asked.

"I'm not with anyone. Just doing a friend a favor."

"Well, tell your friend to get lost." Brendan got up and walked toward the door.

"The Morellis ain't behind this," the man said.

Brendan stopped with his hand on the doorknob.

"They've been working just great with Worley. That's the last thing they want to do is get him in trouble."

"Yet the Mayor was killed in his parking lot," Brendan said.

"Exactly. That's all I've got to say."

"Thanks, pal." Brendan held up his hand to Joe, who looked none too pleased to have brokered the conversation. As Brendan closed the door, he heard Joe say to the guy, "Now beat it."

Brendan went down the street and around the corner to the end of the alley and crouched behind one of the ashcans. A few minutes later, the back door to the luncheonette opened and a stout man in a brown overcoat, hat pulled over his head, looked both ways and walked down the alley in the other direction. There was a car parked a few doors down and Brendan wrote down the license plate. It wasn't much information, but at least he might be able to find out who sent the guy.

Brendan walked back to the station and asked Dominic to come into his office. He picked up the cup of coffee he had left, took a sip of the cold liquid and made a face. Then, still in his overcoat and hat, he reached into the cabinet behind his desk and pulled out a bottle of whiskey and two glasses.

"I believe it's cocktail time," he said and poured them each two fingers.

"What's up?" Dominic said, sitting down in front of the desk.

Brendan removed his hat and coat and sighed.

"Some goon wanted to tell me that the Morellis aren't behind this."

"Gee—you think he was one of them?" Dominic laughed. "That's the most pathetic excuse for a confession."

"That's what I thought, but in a way, it makes sense. If Rob was paying them protection money—"

"What? He was?"

"He didn't specify how much, but he was. Why else would he provide a private room for them to have regular meetings?"

Dominic took a sip of his drink. "I followed up with Vince at the club about who the 'Jones' party was. He hemmed and hawed before admitting that it was very regularly booked by the Morellis."

"So, Vince would know who was making the reservation if he answered the phone. When my brother-in-law took the call, they had to say 'Jones.'"

"How original."

"I don't mean to pry, but isn't there a Barone also connected to the Russo gang?" Brendan asked.

"Yes. But he is no relation to my family. Hey, it's a common name."

"All I know is that the Russos have their own brotherhood trying to muscle into all the illegal stuff the other gangs operate." Dominic stopped short, realizing he had revealed more knowledge that he had previously admitted to.

Brendan looked at him for a moment, aware that Dominic had a large family and many connections in the city. His cousin worked in one of the Morelli stores and his cousin Maria, who had recently wed Detective Clyde Owens, was widowed due to an altercation in a bar. Was it random? Or was her late husband involved in the gang activity? He had wondered how a widow with a young son was able to survive in reduced circumstances. Now, he wondered if the 'family' supported her because of her loss.

"Russo? That's also the name of the folks who own Catalano's," Brendan said.

"Again, a common name."

"Simona works for the Burnsides and she mentioned she had a brother. Now I wonder…"

"Stop wondering and making connections where none exist. Just because we're Italian doesn't mean we have gang connections. Ten years ago, anyone with Irish roots was subject to the same scrutiny."

"Sorry, you're right. But if you could trace this license plate, that might lead us to someone who will talk further. I'd better check in on Rob. What a mess!"

They tipped back the last of their drinks and Brendan made his way to the holding cells. It was an incongruous sight, seeing Rob Worley in his elegant suit sitting among a few homeless men who had probably been arrested for public indecency or intoxication, along with a teenager who looked scared to death. It must have been a calm day, he thought, with so few people there.

As he approached, he asked the officer to let Rob out so they could talk, and it was the first time that he had ever seen a break in the man's confidence.

"You doing okay?" Brendan asked.

"I hope so."

They went into an interview room down the hall. Rob slumped into the chair opposite Brendan.

"If I haven't said it explicitly before, I certainly did not shoot the Mayor. And I believe I am caught in some kind of turf war with the club as the big prize."

"Can you tell me about your relationship with the Morellis?"

"What's to tell? They rent a private room on a regular basis."

"And you pay them protection money?"

"No, I make the room and drinks available at no cost. No money changes hands. I would hardly call it protection money. It's not like they're there all the hours I'm open."

"Maybe not, but if everyone knows they're your friends, that's enough."

"And they're not my friends. It's a simple accommodation."

Brendan sighed. "Do you have a lawyer lined up?"

"Of course. He'll be here shortly with the bail money."

Brendan's eyebrows went up since he was aware of how much that was. But then he remembered that Dominic had told him about the large sack of cash that Rob had deposited the night of the murder, so whatever the amount, he was good for it.

"I'm sure Louisa is taking it hard," Brendan said, making conversation to save Rob from having to sit in a cell with those other folks.

"If there was some way to make things better, I would do it. The Mayor was a good guy as far as I was concerned.

Maybe you don't know, but there are folks who want to come as close to shutting down the alcohol business in this town as when Prohibition was in play."

"You seemed to have done all right back then," Brendan said with a small smile.

"To be honest, I did. Risky business and all, but things worked out," Rob replied.

"I heard your mother got a nice house out of it all. You, too, from what I hear."

Rob shrugged, neither admitting nor denying it.

"You know, there's a group of folks, some of them hotheads, who have been supporting the reduction in hours of the bars. While I would never suggest how you conduct your investigation, it's quite possible that one of them got angry after the Mayor pulled that stunt," Rob said.

Brendan tilted his head, wondering to what stunt he was referring.

"Switching out the agenda item so that Carmichael looked a fool getting all those people at the meeting when there was nothing there for them to concern themselves about."

"Now how do you know that?" Brendan asked.

"Too many people work in City Hall for things to be a secret for long."

"How did it get onto the agenda in the first place, if that's the Mayor's purview?"

"Carmichael had the Fire Marshal authorize a fire drill the

day before so the building would empty and somebody or somebodies switched the paperwork out."

"The Fire Marshal? He was one of O'Hara's friends," Brendan said. "One of his drinking buddies."

"That bunch are all fair-weather friends. Who knows what the new Mayor promised in return for the fire drill? Maybe the Fire Marshal wasn't told what the stakes were or what he was getting into. Or maybe he wants to be Fire Chief."

There was a knock on the door and Herb put his head in. "The attorney is here. Want me to show him in?"

"Sure," Brendan said, all of a sudden having a ridiculous thought that perhaps it would be Mr. Burnside. He had done criminal law way back when, according to Amanda, but had given it up for the more profitable contract law.

Herb ushered in a familiar face, but it wasn't Mr. Burnside. It was one of the patrons Brendan had seen at the Oasis before, usually sitting with a small group of men talking seriously. He wore an expensive overcoat and at the end of what was a long day for Brendan, the man looked as if he had just got out of the barber's chair after a trim and a shave. As he came forward to introduce himself, Brendan caught a whiff of sandalwood, suggesting his assumption might have been correct.

"Will Bishop," he said with a dazzling smile.

"Please sit down."

"Are we in a formal interrogation?" the attorney asked, having put his hand on Rob's shoulder.

"We questioned Mr. Worley at the scene and here at the station, which was more convenient so late at night or early in the morning, I should say. It was only today that the District Attorney saw fit to ask a judge for an arrest warrant."

"Interesting. Had you spoken to Mr. Heller?"

"No. I don't believe I've even met him."

"Do you think he conferred with the Chief before the warrant was issued?"

"I have no idea. You'd have to ask him." Brendan was impressed but not pleased that he was being subjected to the questions.

"I've secured bail for Mr. Worley. And unless there is any further reason to detain him, I believe he can be released." He smiled again.

"I think you are correct." Brendan stood.

The other two men stood as well.

"I understand you and Mr. Worley are acquainted," Will said.

"Yes, we are." Brendan was going to leave it to the attorney to figure it out.

"Nice to meet you," Will said, and shaking Brendan's hand, led his client out the door.

"You'll have some paperwork to sign and they'll return anything they've confiscated from you—money, watch, overcoat and so on," Will informed Rob as they walked down the hall.

Brendan liked Rob Worley and wished him the best even though he was going to go through a rough patch. He just had the feeling that he hadn't been told the whole story.

Chapter 16

The Burnside family was still in chaos with the head of the family berating his daughter for her poor decisions, lack of restraint and terrible choices. Mrs. Burnside and Amanda were both in Louisa's room while this tirade took place and they were not immune from his anger.

"My dear," he admonished his wife, "you've let this one run wild, indulging her every whim."

"That's not true!" she protested. "She did well in school and she's discovered a talent and a job at which she has been successful." Mrs. Burnside sat next to Louisa, who was still propped up in bed, eyes red and puffy from crying.

"She wanted to go to Paris to study design, remember? And you were all for it!" he shouted.

"And Amanda. As her older sister, you could have, might have…"

"Oh, no, Daddy. Don't lay this at my door. You've been

more lenient with her than you were with me. That's what happened. It's not my job to be her jailer."

"Please, everyone will hear," Mrs. Burnside urged. It was hopeless as the staff couldn't avoid the shouting that came from the second floor.

"Can you imagine if she had gone to Paris? Can you?" Mr. Burnside said.

"Well, she didn't, did she?" Amanda said, imagining that her father thought Louisa would have ended up as a can-can dancer in the Moulin Rouge.

"No, she didn't. Instead, she pretended to take classes in social work, remember? Hah! I should have seen through that from the beginning. She wouldn't think of getting her suede pumps sullied by working in the slums! Instead, she was hanging out in a nightclub. During Prohibition when alcohol was still illegal. Sneaking in and out at all hours. Duping us all."

"Edward, please sit down," his wife urged as he was working himself into a full-blown bombastic fit.

He took a breath and sat at the dainty vanity bench and tried to calm himself.

"What's done is done," Amanda said. "You've had Rob here at the house and I think you can agree that the man isn't a cold-blooded killer. He had no argument with the Mayor, who came to the Oasis on a regular basis. Somebody wants a rapid resolution to a high-profile murder and has decided he's the one to hang."

Louisa burst into tears again.

"Sorry, that was a bad choice of words," Amanda said.

There were some moments of silence as Mrs. Burnside patted Louisa's hand.

"The question is, where do we go from here?" Amanda asked. "I know you don't approve of Louisa's relationship with Rob, but she is not involved with this incident. Not even by association. She took a cab home well before Brendan and I left the club." Amanda didn't know that for sure, but at some point, she didn't see her sister seated in the crowd and when she got home, the door to Louisa's bedroom was closed with the light off. They had had a difference of opinion earlier in the evening and she wasn't about to wake up her sister to revisit it nor had she been willing to apologize.

"Is that true?" Mr. Burnside asked.

"Yes!" Louisa said.

Mrs. Burnside let out a sigh. "My suggestion is that we carry on as if nothing is the matter. Louisa, get into some clothes and we'll go downstairs and have a sherry. Then we'll have dinner as we always do and talk about anything but this series of events."

Amanda smiled. "Mother, sometimes I think it's ridiculous that you like to sugar coat things or pretend unpleasantness shouldn't be discussed. But in light of how serious things are—things about which we can do nothing at the moment—I agree with you. Let's try to get back to normal and have dinner."

Mr. Burnside was at the drinks cupboard and poured each of them a large glass of sherry before he poked at the small fire that was lit more for atmosphere than warmth. His wife tried her best to maintain a light conversation about the communications she had had that day with her friends.

"Dorcas said that she nearly ran over a man downtown who dashed across the street. She had to slam on her brakes and almost hit her head on the windshield. I told her she should avoid all that pedestrian traffic—why don't the police do something about jaywalking? It's very dangerous. Then again, I suggested—since she doesn't need a full-time chauffeur—that she take a cab. Much cheaper in the long run."

"The Mayor's funeral is tomorrow," Mr. Burnside said, immediately changing the mood.

"Are you going?" Amanda asked.

"No, I only met the man once. Politicians are not my cup of tea. At least it won't shut most of the city down as it will likely be held in the Cathedral of the Holy Cross." Saying this, he looked at Amanda, and she was sure he was revisiting the unresolved conversation about her marrying a Roman Catholic and if that would cause her to sever ties with her parents.

As they sat down to dinner, Louisa looked at her food and pushed it around on the plate rather than actually eating anything, which caused her parents to exchange glances.

"Perhaps it would be a good idea for you to go into Monsieur Josef's for work tomorrow," Mr. Burnside said.

"Now that Rob has been arrested and they've thrown away the key?" she responded.

"The key has not been thrown away," Amanda interjected, annoyed at her sister's dramatic turn of phrase. "I spoke to Brendan and he was granted bail."

"What does that mean?" Louisa asked. "Does it mean they don't suspect him anymore?"

"It means he has probably put up a great deal of money as a guarantee that he will not flee and will be present for a trial."

"You think he would escape to Canada?" Louisa asked.

"No. First, there is extradition with Canada, so they could send him back. Second, I don't think he wants to forfeit whatever the bail amount is."

"I know he's innocent!" Louisa said.

The rest of the family was silent.

"Do you know who his attorney is?" her father asked.

Louisa shook her head.

"Someone named Will Bishop, Brendan told me," Amanda said.

"He's an up-and-comer, so I've heard. Excellent reputation with criminal law."

Louisa winced at the word 'criminal.'

"I mean, he's in good hands," her father said, softening the blow.

"I think I'd better go up to bed," Louisa said, although Amanda knew she would probably be telephoning Rob while the others were finishing their meal.

As they got up, Cromwell came in and looked up at Mrs. Burnside.

"I imagine he thinks he deserves another walk," she said.

"I'll go with you, Mother," Amanda said and they got their overcoats before retrieving the leash, which always made the dog dance with excitement.

They went down the back stairs and through the garage to the alley but headed to the street instead.

"Why don't you continue through the alley?" Amanda asked.

"Every time we get close to poor Mr. Daugherty's house, he begins to whine. I prefer to take him around to the street in front of his former owner's place, which he doesn't seem to associate with him as much."

"It's sad the way we got him, but he seems to have adjusted well," Amanda said.

They walked slowly as the dog had to sniff every bush and tree trunk and mark them as well.

"You know, I was thinking of difficulties in relationships. When there is a difference in social class or money or even religion," her mother said. "Getting to the altar with your father was not as easy as you might think."

"What? Was he reluctant?"

Her mother laughed. "Not at all. Didn't you ever notice our wedding photo with the maid of honor, best man, groomsmen and bridesmaids?"

"Yes. What of it?"

"There are no photos of my parents in the wedding photos."

"I did notice, but I thought it was the custom for photos to be taken only of the wedding party."

"That's how some people do it. In fact, your grandparents didn't attend the wedding."

Amanda stopped short. "What? Why?"

"As you know, they came from wealth and your father did not. They thought him unsuitable and suspected that he wanted to marry me for my possible inheritance."

"That's ridiculous. And mean, too, as if they suggested you were only worth a possible fortune."

"I agree. I was very angry and, once your father's parents heard of their objections, they also withdrew their support. We had to go it alone. But we managed. We showed them all that a strong bond between two people who love each other can overcome anything." She looked at her daughter with a smile.

While things with Louisa and Rob remained rocky, Amanda got the distinct impression that her mother was expressing approval of her relationship with Brendan. The issue was the practicalities, even though it was something the couple hadn't yet resolved.

The two women had rounded the block and were heading along the sidewalk in front of the Daugherty house.

"Look—there's a For Sale sign," Mrs. Burnside said. "That wasn't there this morning."

"It's a charming house. Four bedrooms that Hugh Van Eaton used to rent out when he lived in the detached house behind. It's also where Mr. Daugherty lived and why Cromwell whines when you pass it. I wonder how much they want for it?"

"What are you thinking? I know you're coming into your inheritance later this year, but don't you think that would be an extravagance? Just look at the size of it."

"But if all the bedrooms were rented out, that would cover the mortgage."

They stood looking at the imposing Tudor-style house while Cromwell was anxious to get going.

"Amanda, I know you and Louisa won't be living with us much longer and I hope your relationships work out the way your father's and mine did. But it seems like time is flying by and I don't know that I'm ready for it."

Amanda linked her arm in her mother's. "Just think if we lived practically around the corner—wouldn't that be fun?"

Chapter 17

Brendan called Amanda early the next morning with an unusual request.

"How'd you like to go to a funeral?"

"Well, isn't that a romantic notion? I assume it's the late Mayor's?"

"You guessed it. The Chief is so skittish about security now since you contacted him about Peabody's fears that he is having most of the force attend. They'll be in their best uniforms, but we detectives will be sprinkled through the crowd, unrecognizable as law enforcement."

"And I'm to be your cover, as they say?"

"Exactly. All you have to do is wear black and block off a few hours of your time starting at ten."

"Hmm. Do you think I could bill the police department for my time?"

Brendan laughed. "Not a chance. But there will be reception after the interment so you'll get a free meal."

"I think I'll pass on the cemetery and the meal, but I'll go to the service."

"Mass. And it will be long."

"What I do for you…" she said. "I'd better take my own car so I can discreetly disappear."

She shared the information with her parents at breakfast, omitting that it was for Brendan's job. Louisa came to the breakfast room still a bit down in the mouth but ready to return to her design job.

"What are you working on now, dear?" her mother asked.

"Mrs. Logan is getting married next month and, of course, being a widow, does not want a white dress. I think she's coming in later today and we'll see if some pastel shade would work."

"I heard it's going to be a small affair," Mrs. Burnside said.

"The late Mr. Logan left her a sizable estate, I understand," Mr. Burnside said. Noting that his family was looking at him, he clarified. "No one in our firm represented the family. I wouldn't share such confidential information. I heard it from someone at the club."

"If you can be ready in a half hour, Louisa, I'll drop you off," Amanda said.

"It won't be too long before I have my own car," Louisa said.

"Really?" Mr. Burnside commented.

"You may think I'm frivolous, but I have been saving every penny that I've earned from my job."

"Well, good for you," her mother said. "Edward, I forgot to tell you that Amanda and I saw a real estate agent's sign in front of the Daugherty house."

"You mean the Van Eaton house."

"Yes, yes, of course. How much do you think they're asking for it?"

"I'm sure the agent was kind enough to have his telephone number listed on the sign."

"I'd better finish getting ready," Amanda said, excusing herself as she left the table.

She would be sure to drive by the house on her way to work and have Louisa jot down the number. Brendan's small apartment would be sufficient for the two of them but owning a house would be much better.

AMANDA THOUGHT she had allowed herself more than enough time to get to the Cathedral of the Holy Cross in South Boston, but traffic was heavy as she began to drive south. She took streets familiar to her: Boylston Street to Tremont and then south near Boston Common. Traffic was slow along this route, and she wondered if the Mayor's funeral was the reason. After a few more blocks, she saw policemen in the intersections holding up east-west traffic to accommodate what looked to be one of the largest public events besides the annual Saint Patrick's Day parade.

Instead of continuing her trajectory, she turned onto a side street about three blocks away and was able to park her car before proceeding on foot. As she drew closer to the Cathedral, it was evident that others had the same thought and the sidewalks had become crowded. She looked at her wristwatch and saw that the funeral was not scheduled to begin for another forty-five minutes, but judging by the turnout, she might not be able to spot Brendan and they might not be able to find a seat.

To her relief, Brendan, standing on the top step looking for her, waved as he spotted her approach.

"I've been here a few hours already," he said. "We had to check the entire building to make sure nobody was lurking but there were already people seated in the pews."

"The traffic just now was so thick and slow moving that I parked over by Shawmut Avenue."

"I'll have to give you a ride back to your car! I didn't realize that Mayor O'Hara was so beloved, judging by the crowds."

"Will we be able to get a seat?" Amanda asked.

"The department has reserved seats for us spread out among the pews. We're supposed to look like a regular couple, but I will tell you that I must remain alert for any potential danger."

"I'll be sure not to distract you too much," she said.

They entered through a gauntlet of police officers in uniform who nodded slightly toward Brendan. Then she gasped as she entered the Cathedral proper with its vaulted ceiling and supporting columns.

"This is huge!" she said, looking toward the altar that seemed to be half a mile away.

Rather than walking down the center aisle, Brendan led her over to the seating on the left of the main aisle.

"We don't get front row seats," he said. "I'm assigned over here. They're going to have Mass, which means communion, which means there will be lines of people, and we might be here longer than I originally anticipated." He ushered her into the pew that was already half full. He sat at the aisle position and they continued their conversation in whispers.

"In our church, we frown on people claiming the aisle seat," Amanda said. "But folks like to sit there so they can make a fast escape. I used to find it annoying when some gentlemen would do that and instead of moving down the pew, they make a scene of being peeved and take their time getting up and stepping into the aisle before you can get in. Worse are the large men who just stand up and you have to sidle in between them and the pew in front."

"When I was a kid, my mother used to like to sit in one of the aisle pews and I preferred it since I couldn't wait to get up and go home for something to eat. You know, we're not supposed to eat from midnight until after communion," he said.

"I didn't know that. How awful for young children."

"That's why we always went to early Mass. I envied my friends who were Protestant and could go to church leisurely on Sunday, or not. We had to attend. Mandatory."

"I see you use the past tense. Do you still go?"

"Sometimes."

"Aha, a chink in the armor!" she said. "One point for me."

"What do you mean?"

"You can hardly claim that your religion is so important to you, yet disregard the rules that go with it. I am not obligated to attend church each Sunday, but it is the rare occasion that I don't."

"All right. You win that point. But give me time and I'll think of a counter argument."

She smiled. "And I seem to remember you eating meat one Friday when we had lunch."

"You must be wrong. I would never."

"Perhaps not in front of your mother and father or Father Patrick. Look, there's Dominic," she said. He had walked up the central aisle, paused, genuflected and crossed himself before getting into a pew, also seated on the aisle.

They stopped conversing, which gave Amanda the opportunity to admire the stained glass windows that lined the side walls, giving plenty of natural light although the giant chandeliers had been lit. Somber organ music began as the cathedral filled up and it looked as though it might be standing room only.

Finally, after what seemed like hours, the widow O'Hara, dressed in black with a black veil that reached to mid-calf, entered on the arm of her son, Kenny Deegan, looking appropriately somber.

Brendan leaned over to Amanda and whispered, "I wonder what will become of his job at Hudson's?"

She looked quizzically at him.

"It's a job the late Mayor got for his stepson. Sounds like it was either in return for a favor or for a possible future favor. I'd better stop talking and pay attention now," he added as he scanned the area in front of him and to the side.

Some minutes passed and the organ music changed, some bells chimed and everyone stood up as the priest and his attendants entered from a side room so far from where Amanda and Brendan sat that they seemed quite small. To her mind, the Mass consisted of a lot of standing and kneeling accompanied by chimes ringing before finally being able to sit down. The priest moved over to the pulpit and read a passage from the Gospel and then sat down. The Chief got up from one of the front pews and ended up at the pulpit, where he cleared his throat before delivering a passionate eulogy.

"This man. This brave man. Cut down in the prime of life. Leaving a grieving widow and son. Why does this happen? Why does God let this happen?" The Chief proceeded to drift into a long explanation about why God let bad things happen and what good things the rest of us could take from it. He ended with some strong words, however. "Whoever did this will pay. Whoever took this good man who gave so much to this city before his time will be caught and will pay in the strongest possible way. I pledge to you that I will see this done. Mayor O'Hara was a close friend of mine and a precious asset to the community. I will see that his memory is protected and cherished."

Brendan looked around and whispered to Amanda, "That sounded like a campaign speech, not a eulogy."

"Do you think that's what's on his mind?"

"I wouldn't put it past him. He's got a high profile and he knows that Carmichael can seem cold. Not a good look in a politician, much less a Mayor."

"Did you notice any of the gang people come in?" she asked.

"No, but both the Morellis and Russos gave large floral arrangements." He lifted his chin to indicate the garish pieces on either side of the altar.

"Oh, my. At least they are not lucky horseshoes or shamrocks," she said.

Brendan bit his lip to suppress a smile. "It does make me wonder if they worked with O'Hara or would like everyone to think they did or if they're just good people mourning their lost leader. Perhaps a little bit of each."

The last bit of standing occurred, followed by the blessing on the congregation, before the widow and her son walked down the center aisle toward the exit. She looked tiny and bereft beside Kenny, and Amanda turned to look at Brendan and whispered, "He doesn't look very sad about things."

"Things are about to get much better for him. If the Mayor had a hefty life insurance policy and his widow has a portion of his pension benefits, the finances are stable. And she dotes on the boy—man, I should say. No more dirty looks from the stepfather urging him to apply himself."

"A motive?" Amanda asked.

Brendan only shrugged.

Chapter 18

Amanda went back to work and Brendan attended the interment along with half the police force watching intently for who was there and who wasn't. Mayor Carmichael had a sour look on his face, having been overlooked to make any sort of eulogy even though it was well-known that he and O'Hara were not best of friends. He was particularly annoyed that the Chief beat the law-and-order drum, which was something he wanted to emphasize about his administration in his speech at the Council meeting. He had been pre-empted, but now he controlled the agenda and the ordinance about early closing of the bars was coming up for a vote. He went up to Mrs. O'Hara and shook her hand with both of his, aware that several photographers had come to the gravesite and he was likely to be on the front pages of the newspapers again.

Carmichael stepped back to where Henry Rogers, relieved that the new Mayor had acknowledged his skills and contacts, stood. He had made immediate contact with

Carmichael after he learned of O'Hara's death and, while some might have considered that opportunistic, it served both well. Henry's migration brought along Bill, the legislative aide, and Paul, whose specialty was constituent services. Poor Mrs. Derwin had not been asked to join the new Mayor and was now relegated to a lesser position in the Clerk's office; Carmichael had chosen someone from the Councilors' secretarial pool to join the group. She was not as experienced as Mrs. D., but she was bright and younger and the new mayor thought she conveyed the image of an end of the old guard and a new start.

Brendan stood back from those assembled graveside, watching as people moved away from the widow and jockeyed to get near Carmichael. The priest said his blessing, the coffin was lowered and the crowd began to disperse. Kenny escorted his mother to a waiting limousine and then came back to those still standing around and shook hands with as many as he could. Then he walked over to Brendan and thanked him for coming.

"This has been terrible for my mother and me. But I thought I might be able to help you with your investigation."

"How's that?" Brendan asked.

"An old friend of my stepdad's is interested in talking to you."

"When?"

"I've lost my ride. Why don't you drive and I'll give the directions."

"Don't you have to help your mother at the reception?"

"She can wait."

Brendan gave him a hard look. "What is this about? It sounds like a set-up."

"It's anything but," Kenny answered.

Once in the car, Brendan asked, "Where to?"

"There's a restaurant a couple of blocks from here. Just go out the gates and turn left onto Mount Auburn Street and then right on Belmont."

Brendan drove and at one point glanced over to see if there was a gun bulge in Kenny's suit jacket, but he had on an overcoat and it could be concealed. He thought he was insane to have agreed to go with the man, but it was broad daylight and it was a populated area. Then he had to chuckle to himself as that meant nothing if something nefarious was already in play.

"There," Kenny said pointing to a small storefront restaurant with *Palermo* scrawled in elaborate gilded cursive over the front door. Brendan parked and looked around to see pedestrians on the street and a woman wheeling a baby carriage. All very normal.

Kenny led the way inside to a space not unlike Catalano's except it was lunchtime and there were no customers, only a man at the cash register just inside the front door. He nodded to Kenny and went back toward what was probably the kitchen. Brendan took off his hat and Kenny guided him to a booth along the wall under a mural that depicted Palermo's crescent-shaped bay with a mountain in the background.

"Do you want something to eat?" Kenny asked.

"No, thank you," Brendan answered.

The man from the cash register came from the back of the restaurant carrying a tray with a bottle of wine and two glasses.

"Thanks," Kenny said, standing up. Another man had appeared next to him: medium height, dark hair and expensive suit. "This is Tony."

Brendan recognized him as one of the men that frequented the private room at the Oasis.

The man stuck out his hand. "Tony Morelli," he said with a pleasant smile. He sat down.

Kenny said, "I'll catch a cab," and left.

It was just the two of them in an empty restaurant, which felt weird to Brendan but not as intimidating as he might have thought.

"Take off your coat—have a drink with me."

Brendan wiggled out of his overcoat.

"I've seen you at Oasis," he said. "It's a shame about O'Hara. He was a stand-up guy." He poured a glass of red wine for Brendan and then one for himself. They raised their glasses in a toast and took a sip. This was not the usual cheap wine served. This was robust and smooth.

"Are we toasting the late Mayor?" Brendan asked.

"Why not? I would have liked to have been at the funeral, but sometimes I draw the wrong kind of attention. After all, I'm just a businessman but people have their prejudices about me."

There were a few moments of silence before Brendan asked, "Why did you want to meet with me?"

"I'd like to help you find out who killed the Mayor."

"That's a generous offer, but I don't see how you can help."

Tony laughed out loud. "Please. I have folks everywhere. They hear and see things that you cannot."

"What have they heard?"

"It's the Russo gang."

"I'm not surprised you say that considering that they are your rivals."

Tony held out his hands, palms up, to indicate that was an unjust accusation. "I'm a businessman—he's a businessman. We're not rivals. There's plenty of opportunities for everyone. It's not like a cannoli and there are only so many bites. Success breeds success and more opportunities."

"For loan sharking, numbers running and theft. Need I go on?"

Tony was shaking his head with a smile. "I own this place and many other restaurants and bars in the city. I admire Rob Worley for the success that he has had with the Oasis. And so do the Russos. They've wanted to take over his business for some time and he's always said no. And now they've forced the issue by this recent incident. All fingers point in their direction."

"You're forgetting about José Guzmán. He's the silent partner and from what I hear, the majority owner."

"Phsst," Tony said, waving his hand. "He was. Rob bought him out some time ago. They like to pretend the arrangement hasn't changed. Guzmán likes to act like a big shot, but why is he still living with his wife's family? His family lost everything in the last coup back home. Rob has been slowly buying him out and that's what he lives on."

"Until the next revolution."

"Exactly."

"So, you're saying the Russos are behind this? They killed the Mayor?"

Tony gave an exaggerated shrug. "Sounds like what they would do."

"I am not getting in the middle of a gang war," Brendan said, sliding out of the booth and putting on his overcoat.

"There's no war and there's not going to be one. I'm just offering my help in gathering information. We can work together."

"Thank you for the wine. And the conversation," Brendan said and left. He took a deep breath of air once he was out on the sidewalk but didn't want to linger or relax his guard. He got in his car and mulled over what had just taken place. What was it? Was the Russo gang behind it or was it the Morelli gang? Either one would have been fine to set Rob up and take over the lucrative business. How was Kenny involved with the Morellis? Was he trying to give them some legitimacy or get a job with them, something more interesting than working at Hudson's? Was he hoping to be the new face and proprietor of the Oasis? Too many undercurrents were at work in his brain as well as the full glass of wine on an empty stomach. He stopped at the nearest delicatessen, ordered a grinder at the counter and sat down to think it over.

~

BRENDAN WAS WALKING toward the station when he heard rapid footsteps behind him so he moved out of the way, but the man sidled up to him instead.

"You Halloran?"

"Who wants to know?" Brendan asked.

"Someone thinks you need to hear both sides of things?"

"What things?" He knew full well that he must be one of Russo's people trying to cover their tracks.

"Can we talk somewhere more private?" the man said, looking all around.

"Sure. The station's just up there. We can go into an interview room."

"Very funny."

"Okay, let's go to Joe's luncheonette. It's just around the corner." He knew that the answer would be 'no' as well.

"There's a better place just up ahead," the man said.

"Are you sure? Joe serves a great cup of coffee." Seeing the pained look on the man's face, he agreed to accompany him to the crowded cafeteria where many downtown workers went. They didn't get in the service line but sat in a corner booth with the man facing away from the diners. Brendan put his hat on the seat beside him but didn't take off his overcoat, showing his impatience for this chat to be over quickly.

"So?" Brendan asked.

"The Russos had nothing to do with this business."

"What business might that be?"

"Stop pulling my leg. You know. The Mayor and all."

"The shooting of the Mayor was bad enough. What is the 'and all' to which you refer?"

"The fallout as a result. The crackdown on innocent Italian men trying to earn a living."

"If you call loan sharking and numbers running innocent, then I would agree with you. But some of your compatriots are involved in rougher things than that—things I probably can't imagine."

The man looked down at his thick fingers resting on the tabletop. "Is there anything I can do for you?"

Brendan couldn't believe the man was being so obvious. "Look, I'm being bombarded with trying to pin it on the other side."

"You folks probably don't make very much. I've seen your car. You could probably get a newer one. I know a guy."

Brendan just stared at him.

"Okay. Also, I've seen where you live. One side of a dinky duplex. You should be living in a big house since you'll be getting married soon."

Brendan still said nothing.

"Well, anyway, think about it."

"I have thought about it and you're lucky we're not sitting at Joe's where I would be free to sock you in the nose. I wouldn't waste his excellent coffee throwing it at you."

The man shrugged and got up. Brendan remained seated, fuming at the audacity and concerned that he seemed to know a lot about his life. He was more concerned that Amanda had been brought into the equation. Now both Burnside sisters were drawn into the world of crime, intimidation and murder.

Brendan picked up his hat and placed it roughly on his head, determined to move this case along before he had any more well-intentioned talks with random men or an all-out gang war erupted. He stormed into the station with such a look of determination and disgust on his face that everyone in his path gave him wide berth. He finally sat at his desk and shook his head to clear it of the jumble of thoughts when Herb stuck his head around the corner of the open office door.

"That guy who's been in to see you before is here again."

"That's helpful. Does 'that guy' have a name or a reason to be seeing me?"

"Smith or something. And, no, he didn't tell me what he wanted."

"Send him in," Brendan said waving his hand in surrender.

Herb left and reappeared a few minutes later with Symington. "Here he is."

Brendan suppressed a groan at seeing the man with the pile of papers under his arm, the topmost ones bent back from constant friction. He knew exactly what the man wanted to talk about and he did not invite him to sit, thinking that Symington would tire of standing reciting the same issues as before and leave more quickly.

"Have you found out who shot the Mayor?" he asked.

"I can't comment on an ongoing case. Is that why you're here?"

"No. I'm here because the same after-hours activity is going on at all the bars, clubs and taverns in town."

"All? Have you been to all of them to monitor their activity?"

"Not all, of course. But the same offenders. I can't believe that you allowed the Oasis to reopen so they can get up to the same shenanigans as before! And this new Mayor is no better than the last."

"I can't speak to his performance since he hasn't had much time in the job. But I'm surprised you didn't know that the ordinance having those establishments close at midnight will be in front of the Mayor and Council soon."

Symington scowled. "I was just at City Hall looking for a posted agenda. It wasn't up. How did you know?"

"A contact in the Clerk's office," Brendan said although it had been Amanda who had told him. "It'll be up soon, I imagine."

Without giving his thanks or saying goodbye, Symington scuttled out of the office and down the hall. Brendan wished he had thought of that technique in prior visits, but it wasn't fiction. Amanda had got the information from Nora. He wondered if he should attend that meeting and see if any interesting characters showed up.

Herb appeared again at the open door. "Sorry, sir. Someone here to see you."

"Another Smith?"

"To be honest, that's what this guy said his name was."

"Put him in interview room number one so I can escape as needed."

Brendan hauled himself out of his chair, taking a notebook and a pencil with him, wondering if he would get anything done that day.

A heavy-set man with thinning hair came in and introduced himself as John Smith.

Brendan couldn't resist saying, "Is that really your name?"

"Sure thing," the man said, pulling out a wallet from a back pocket and producing a driver's license with that name.

"Okay. Sorry, long day already. Please, sit down."

"I think I have to report something."

"Really?"

"Yes. I have a hauling business right across the street from the Oasis although access is from the side street. My wife and I have an apartment right above."

Brendan sat up straighter.

"A few days ago, I was up early in the morning getting ready for a long haul when I heard a shot. I woke up my wife and she said she didn't hear anything. But then I heard someone running."

"From which direction?"

"I couldn't tell. We have blackout curtains because of my hours. And when I got back from this job that took me up to Maine, the missus tells me that the Mayor was shot right across the street. She says the cops were there and an ambulance. So, I thought I should tell someone about it."

"I didn't think anyone lived across the street," Brendan said.

"The entries are on the side streets or the street behind. You wouldn't think anybody lived there from the outside."

"What else can you tell me?"

"That's about it. Except that guy that just left—I've seen him before. Hanging around on the street late at night."

"Symington?" Brendan asked.

"I didn't talk to him. I just peered out through a crack in the blackout curtains from time to time to see the activity at the Oasis. I've never been in there myself. Probably too highbrow and expensive."

"Does the noise from the club bother you?"

"It's not noisy from the outside. When they close for the night, the whole street is quiet."

"Can you give me your phone number?"

"Sure," the man said and wrote it in Brendan's notebook.

"We may be in touch again."

"That's okay. I'm sometimes gone for a day or two on a job, but otherwise, I'm here."

Brendan shook the man's hand. "Thank you for your help."

He escorted John Smith to the exit and passed Dominic on his way back to his office.

"Things just got interesting. If what that man heard was correct, it wasn't a shot fired from a car. It was someone on foot. That points away from gang involvement and back to one of several people who were in the area. Rob Worley, Vince Renard and possibly Symington."

Chapter 19

Amanda called just as he was finishing up for the day. "How about dinner at my house?"

"That would be wonderful. I hadn't planned that far ahead."

"I did want to talk to you someplace other than a church where we had to whisper. And we'd be glad to have you—Cook thinks you're Prince Charming—although I don't know why. And having someone for dinner will tone down the conversation."

"What conversation?"

"My father railing about and at Louisa. Regarding Rob and the Oasis business."

"So you're inviting me as a buffer for your father's justified furor at all the negative attention his younger daughter has drawn to herself?"

"Yes. Is that a problem? I will return the favor someday as you have three younger siblings. My father won't hector her and it will be a pleasant meal until Louisa excuses herself early to call Rob. A strictly forbidden contact that she makes at home on the Q.T. and now from work where there are no impediments."

"Thank goodness we don't face such obstacles," Brendan said.

"That's because you uphold the law for a living," Amanda said.

"And Rob skates on the edge and is filthy rich as a result. I'll be over early and I'll update you if you have information for me."

Brendan got to the Burnside home before Amanda's father, who had insisted on picking up Louisa from work. For some reason he thought that ferrying her to and from work would impede her ability to talk to Rob. Louisa managed to look down in the mouth when her father appeared, as though she had been complying with his edict, all the while relishing the fact that she could call Rob and have long conversations from the telephone at Monsieur Josef's salon.

Upon being ushered inside, Brendan inhaled deeply. "Oh, what's for dinner?"

"Cook has conjured up sauerbraten with spaetzle and red cabbage. Had she known earlier that you were coming, she might have been tempted to make corned beef and cabbage."

"It's a good thing she didn't as it couldn't compare to my sainted mother's."

"Said like a loyal son. Here, let me put your hat and coat away," Amanda said after receiving a kiss on the cheek.

Once in the sitting room, she poured them both a glass of sherry, the usual before-dinner drink in the household.

"Now, what have you got to tell me about the case?" She crossed one leg over the other to face him more fully.

"I know everything and nothing. The information keeps flooding in and it makes me no wiser."

"That's not very hopeful."

"I should tell you that the Morelli and Russo folks are nervous because they keep sending people to tell me that it wasn't their folks who did the Mayor in. And it might surprise you—or not—that one of those folks who arranged for a meeting was Kenny Deegan."

"Oh, that is interesting. Now, how do you think he is involved? And what do you imagine he brings to the equation?"

"That's an interesting point. Perhaps he was the go-between for the late Mayor and the Morellis. Which is a bit odd because I got the impression that O'Hara and his stepson didn't think highly of each other."

"Politics makes strange bedfellows?" Amanda said.

"Perhaps. What did Kenny get out of it? He already had a nominal job although some cash may have come his way as a result. He couldn't afford to openly be working with the Morellis or his stepfather's reputation and Kenny's gravy train would have come to a halt."

"Maybe it made him feel like a big shot. He lived his life in the shadow of a big man in more ways than one."

They each sipped the sherry while considering the implications.

"Kenny arranged the meeting but didn't participate. It was a smooth-talking older man in a very expensive suit."

"Sounds like someone important. I gather you didn't exchange calling cards."

"No."

"Who was the other contact?"

"Just some guy," Brendan said. "A thug. It seems he was asked to do a job by talking or threatening me and he wasn't subtle in doing so. And once I told him to beat it, he didn't seem to be bothered."

"You told a gangster to beat it?" Amanda asked, wide-eyed. "You could have been killed!"

"As you can see, I'm still here. Besides, we were in that cafeteria downtown with scores of people, so not a conducive location for a mob hit."

"Brendan! Don't joke—this is really serious. Obviously, someone already used assassination as a remedy although we don't know what the problem was that needed to be fixed. If they didn't hesitate at killing the Mayor, what difference would one police detective be?"

"Even if he is a Lieutenant and the head of the division?" he asked, hoping to lighten the mood.

"That's not remotely amusing." She turned away in annoyance.

"Okay, what did you learn today?"

"Absolutely nothing of relevance. After the funeral, I had lunch and went to a bank and had the tedious job of looking through someone's deposits and withdrawals and was none the wiser when I finished. Some people are either very honest or extremely adept at hiding their assets."

"Ah—the divorce case."

"How did you guess?"

"Once we're married, you won't have to ever worry about that. I own a car, some clothes and a small savings account."

"That will never do," Amanda said.

"It will prevent me from being killed for my money, that's for sure. Although there is a pension with the job that would go to the widow."

"Your sense of humor is perverted. As it happens, I'm about to come into some money."

Brendan laughed. "Rich uncle or some boyfriend I don't know about?"

"Kind grandparents who thought ahead."

That silenced Brendan. "Really?"

She nodded. "They were very sweet people."

"Would it be crass, even though I am your fiancé, to inquire how much that might be?"

She looked in the eye and told him.

"Oh, my," he said.

"Yes."

"You've suddenly made me uncomfortable," Brendan said in all seriousness.

"What do you mean? You could see my parents were well off."

"But I didn't know that you were a woman of independent means, as they say."

"Is that a problem now?"

"Not at all, my dear. I expect you to treat me to the best life ever."

She swatted him on the arm. "Can't you talk about this seriously?"

"I'd love to. What shall we buy?"

She scanned his face to judge his state of mind. "I was thinking that some could be used for a downpayment on a house."

His eyebrows raised. "I like that idea. I like it very much." He leaned forward to kiss her just as they heard the sound of her mother's high heels in the entry to the sitting room and they pulled apart.

"Hello, you two! I'm glad you've come to dinner, Brendan. Things have been tense here lately."

"Yes, Amanda told me and it seems I am to be the light diversion or something."

"Those two! I'm as upset about the situation as anyone. But they seem to enjoy engaging in dramatic scenes and, frankly, I am getting exhausted."

"A sherry might perk you up," Brendan said, getting up to pour a drink for her.

"When will we see an end to all this?" Mrs. Burnside said, sitting in one of the armchairs.

"It's a long process. We're still gathering evidence, and I wish there was something conclusive, but we're a long way off from resolving things."

"Is Rob still in jail?" she asked.

"I guess Louisa didn't tell you, he posted bail and he's been released. He's not supposed to leave the jurisdiction, but he can continue his work at the Oasis."

"I suppose that's a relief. He didn't have to close down the nightclub?"

"The ABC Commission always looks into situations where someone is killed on the premises of a business, but the Mayor was killed in the parking lot, which is not the same thing as operating a rowdy environment with constant violence or fights."

Mrs. Burnside's eyes grew wide. "Oh, my. I suppose there are such places."

"Yes, indeed. I'm sorry to say there are some men who get a kick out of having too much to drink and starting a fight. Just like in the Western movies. The Oasis, as you saw when you visited, is not that sort of place. The Commission will take that into consideration and probably allow him to continue to operate."

"I suppose that's a good thing," she said.

"This may sound strange, but rather than business being off, it was packed last night from what I hear."

"That's awful," Amanda said. "As if people are ghouls to enjoy such a thing."

"I can't speak to what the motivations of the crowd were, but the name of the club was plastered across the front pages of every newspaper in town. Folks may have driven by to see if it was one of those wild places and found themselves surprised that it looks and is an elegant club with good food, legal liquor and entertainment. Rob Worley gives the place a certain level of class that people don't always expect."

Mrs. Burnside smiled slightly, evidently not exactly agreeing with the sentiment that Brendan had expressed. To her mind, class was less about exterior appearances and more about values and she often questioned Rob's based on where he grew up as well as the profession he had chosen.

There was a clatter as Mr. Burnside and Louisa came into the sitting room via the back stairs and the kitchen. They both looked out of sorts with grim faces and only brightened up when they saw the others having a pleasant chat.

"Well, hello, Brendan," Mr. Burnside said, shaking his hand after he had stood up.

"Rough day at work, Daddy?" Amanda asked, hoping to get his mind off the family situation.

"It was very productive as we interviewed some fine young men for a position at the firm. You know, Amanda, you are just as bright as any of them and it would be swell if you would think about joining the law."

He took Louisa's coat and went to the closet beside the vestibule, hung it up and then his own, before returning to the group.

Brendan's head swiveled in her direction. "I didn't know you were considering that."

"I'm not. Daddy has been trying to plant the seed that it would suit my skills and personality."

"He's not wrong," Brendan said. "Are you ready to embark upon three years of law school?"

Amanda sighed at the prospect of such a journey.

"That's not the only way, although it is becoming the standard these days. Why, consider Abraham Lincoln, who 'read the law' under the mentorship of a licensed attorney."

"The law has gotten a lot more complex these days, I suspect," Amanda said.

"It's still a viable way to study. In fact, more practical in that you are seeing real cases from the outset, not just reading textbooks. You've already had a taste of it and you have an innate sense of critical thinking."

"Not just yet, Edward," Mrs. Burnside said, hoping to keep her girls home with them as long as possible. She had overlooked the fact that they were already out in the world earning a living.

The doorbell rang and they continued to sit, expecting one of the maids to answer it.

Finally, Louisa said, "I'll get it. They're busy in the kitchen helping Cook with this feast."

She opened the vestibule door and then the front door but saw no one. There was a box on the mat and she brought it in.

"Who was there?" her father asked.

"Nobody. Just this lovely box."

She showed them the powder blue box tied with a white ribbon.

"I wonder who it's for?" Amanda asked. "It looks expensive. In which case, I'll arm wrestle you for it."

That made them all laugh since that had been their way to settle disputes when they were younger although nobody remembered how it had originated.

"Just open it and we'll argue about it afterward," Amanda said.

Louisa sat down and undid the bow and took off the lid. She stared at the contents for a moment before dropping the box and letting out a shriek. A bullet rolled out from the tissue paper onto the rug.

"Don't touch it!" Brendan said, taking a handkerchief from his pocket and picking up the bullet. "I don't know for whom this was meant, but I'll get it tested for prints."

"This has gone too far, Louisa. Now the entire family has become embroiled because of your dalliance with that man. And for all we know, he might have committed the murder."

"Rob can't have done it. I was with him the entire time at the club," Louisa said.

"No, you weren't. You went home early," Amanda said.

"That's what I told you, but I didn't go home. I did have a headache and I went upstairs to Rob's office. You can see and hear the whole place from there. He's got a couch and I lay down on it and dozed off. When I woke up, there were still some people in the club and it wasn't closing time yet. Rob came up to check on me, and I told him I felt better. I was going to stay up there until everyone left and then he would give me a ride home."

Amanda crossed her arms over her chest and looked at her sister skeptically.

"It was totally above board. After all, we're engaged."

"Oh, great," Amanda said, realizing that Louisa had not been joking about it previously.

Mrs. Burnside burst into tears and her husband gave Louisa a withering look. "When did this happen?"

"Several weeks ago."

"Did you know about this?" he asked Amanda.

"I only found out the other day. You know I hate being in the middle of her escapades."

"It's not an escapade. We love each other."

Her father had some difficulty being heard over the sobs of his wife. "And he didn't think to come to me to ask my permission?"

"Daddy, that's so old hat," Louisa said.

"I suppose you think locking up one's daughter is old hat, too? It's exactly what's going to happen now."

Louisa was defiant but had begun to cry.

"Where was Rob then?" Brendan asked, trying to bring everyone back to the task at hand.

Louisa took a handkerchief and dabbed her eyes. "I could see him moving around the club, saying a word to one waiter or another until all the tables were cleared, tablecloths removed and the staff left one by one. Only Vince was left. Rob came back up and told me he was going to count up the take and fill out a deposit slip."

"The take?" Amanda asked. Somehow that phrase made Mrs. Burnside let out a groan.

"How much they made that night. The bills were already sorted into denominations by Frank and totaled. Rob just needed to check the count, which he did. He put the money back in the safe and went back downstairs to see if Vince was still there. They sat and chatted while Vince smoked a cigarette, which I could see through the window. Finally, Vince left, and Rob picked up the ashtray, took it away to the kitchens, then came back into the main room to do his last-minute checking that nobody was in one of the restrooms. That's when Vince came crashing through the door."

"What did you do?"

"I waited for Rob to come upstairs to ask him what the matter was. He told me and decided to call you, Brendan. You advised him to call the station to report what Vince had seen. He said to go into the private bathroom in his office and stay there. He was gone a long time as I guess you all got there and then an ambulance. I sneaked out at one point and through the window up above I could see you talking to Rob and Vince. It seemed to take forever. Then he got up and I suspected he was coming back upstairs, but I could hear two voices so I went back into the bathroom. The other detective—"

"Dominic," Brendan supplied.

"Yes, Dominic, used the phone to call a towing company. I could hear the safe being opened and closed and then they both went down the steps. Rob stopped and I heard him say he forgot the deposit slip and came back upstairs. He told me to just wait there, that I'd be perfectly safe and he'd be back to take me home. He said it might be a while, so I lay down on the couch and fell asleep."

"And then?" Mr. Burnside asked.

"He finally came back before dawn and drove me home. I got here long before Cook came in."

"Speaking of Cook, I'm sure she could hear all the commotion here and didn't dare disturb the drama to tell us dinner was ready." Amanda stood up, hoping to encourage the others to do the same.

"I'm not hungry," Louisa said.

"Fine, go to bed without dinner. Relieve your mother and me of worry for once. I, for one, am hungry, Brendan? Dear?" he addressed his wife before adding, "You're not going to starve because of all this. Come on." He held out his hand to help her from her seat and she followed him into the dining room.

"This case has got to come to a close soon," Brendan said to Amanda.

"Amen to that!"

Chapter 20

Mayor Carmichael had settled in easily to the job he had set his eyes on with the added assistance of the former Mayor's staff. When he was a Council Member, he had to share secretarial help, and his one aide was transferred to his newly appointed replacement. The meeting the next day would catapult him to the front pages again when he made his speech about tackling crime and cleaning up the city, bolstered by the ordinance changing closing hours of bars, clubs and taverns that was to be presented.

He was just editing the wording of the last sentence when his assistant, Miss Johnstone, knocked on the door and put her head around it.

"There's a telephone call from somebody who represents the Food and Beverage Association."

"What? I mean, who is it?"

She looked down at the slip of paper in her hand. "Mr. Selby. He wants to meet with you as soon as possible."

"Find a time day after tomorrow," Carmichael said.

"I think he meant today."

The Mayor let out a puff of frustration. She still stood there expectantly while he looked at his watch.

"Okay."

She left and came back a few minutes later with another slip of paper on which was written an address that she handed him.

"What's this?"

"He'd like you to meet him at the Parker House at five-thirty."

Carmichael let out another sigh of impatience. "I really prefer meetings to take place here. Call him back and have him come here then instead."

She shifted from one foot to the other. "He didn't leave his phone number."

Mrs. Derwin wouldn't have made that rookie mistake, he thought. "I'll go. But in future, all meetings here."

"Yes, sir," she said and slipped out of the room.

At least it would be the cocktail hour and the man had better buy him a drink, maybe even dinner. First, he wanted to end his speech with a punchy line that people would remember. It could also be incorporated into a slogan when campaign time came up. He pushed the button on the intercom and said, "Miss Johnstone, is Henry Rogers here?" Upon hearing that he was, he asked her to have him come to his office.

"You wanted to see me, boss?" Henry said a few minutes later when he came in without knocking.

"A little protocol to begin with. Please knock, don't just waltz in. Next, don't call me boss. It makes me sound like a mobster. 'Mayor' or 'Your Honor' will do."

"Sure thing," Henry said.

"Sit, sit. I'm working on a speech. No, it's more of an introduction to the proposed ordinance. And I need a phrase that could almost be a slogan that relates to it."

"Which ordinance?" Henry asked, knowing there were several on the agenda for the next evening.

Carmichael put his hands up in frustration. "The closing hours one."

"Sure." Henry put out his hand and ticked off on his fingertips the various appropriate slogans. "How about 'Safer Streets,' 'Protect Our Communities,' 'People over Profits,' 'Smart Limits,' 'Families First' or 'Curb the Sale?'"

The Mayor was astonished at Henry's quick mind and delivery and asked him to repeat them as he wrote them down. "I don't like 'Curb the Sale' because people will think we're trying to ram prohibition down their throats. 'Safer Streets' is good. Very good. It will apply to some other policies I'm thinking about relating to crime."

Henry sat waiting for the next request.

"That's all. Say, someone from the Food and Beverage Association is meeting with me in less than an hour."

Henry's eyes widened. "Did he say what it was about?"

"No. I think you'd better come to the meeting with me."

"Sure thing," Henry said and left.

He returned shortly with a file folder and handed it to the Mayor.

"What's this?"

"Information about the group. They're sort of a guild of restaurant owners, bars, clubs and taverns. They want to protect their businesses. This will be a rough meeting, I'm afraid."

Having dealt mostly with ordinary constituents previously, Mayor Carmichael nervously looked at the list of names that were linked to all the large hotels, private and public clubs and bars in Boston. He was impressed.

"Well, it's only one man. Let's get going then," the Mayor said.

They walked the short distance in a matter of minutes and entered the wood-paneled lobby with its enormous chandelier.

Henry leaned in close to Carmichael. "That's him over there."

A large man got up from a chair in front of one of the enormous wooden columns and smiled as he approached.

Holding out his hand, he said, "What a pleasure to meet you in person, Your Honor."

"Thank you. Always good to get to know the business community."

"Henry," the man nodded in the aide's direction.

"Mr. Selby," he nodded in return.

"I'll take your coat and hat to the cloakroom," Henry offered.

"Thank you, and then you can go," Carmichael said.

Henry hesitated for a moment and said, "Thank you."

"You're a lifelong Bostonian so surely you know the bar," Selby said.

"Oh, yes. Glamorous place."

The two men walked side by side down a hallway to the bar that had a handful of men, some standing alone and several in pairs engaged in conversation.

"What will you have?" Selby asked. "I'm a bourbon drinker, myself."

"That would be fine, thank you."

"Please, find a table and I'll get the drinks," Selby said, going up to the bartender.

"Two double bourbons," Selby said.

Returning with the drinks a few minutes later, he smiled as he sat down opposite the Mayor. "I expect you'll want to know all about the Food and Beverage Association."

"I'm sure that will be fascinating," Carmichael said as they touched glasses in a toast.

Selby started his dissertation with the fateful phrase, "It all started a long time ago."

He began with the early settlement of New England and held forth on the differences between taverns, inns, alehouses, pubs and taprooms that took him at least twenty minutes. The Mayor sipped his drink and managed to look attentive although he was mightily bored. By the time Selby got to the Mexican American War, the Mayor's glass was empty.

"Here, let me get you a refill," Selby said, getting up quickly before his guest could protest. The Mayor was already feeling the effects of the first drink so he told himself to slow down on the next one. Perhaps they would move into the dining room where food would cancel the effects of alcohol on an empty stomach, Minutes later, Selby came back, sat down and began where he left off.

Carmichael had never met anyone so talkative that he hardly seemed to breathe between sentences so there was no opportunity to break in or ask a question. Halfway through the second drink Selby suddenly stopped and stood.

"Come on," he beckoned. "Let's go to the dining room. We may meet some folks who are the backbone of the Association who add millions to the City of Boston's budget each year. Restaurateurs whose cuisine is so well known that tourists come to our fair city just to eat here. Bars, like the one we've just been in, where commerce is conducted, clubs with dancing and entertainment that provides the livelihood for thousands of people. The local tavern, where the honest working man can go in the evening and listen to the fights on the radio with his neighbors. Now, you wouldn't want to undercut the work of all those people—people with families to support and rents to pay, would you?"

They had reached the double doors of one of the meeting

rooms on the first floor and Selby pulled them open and announced, "Mayor Carmichael."

A flashbulb made a popping sound and the large group of men assembled in the room were silent. The Mayor realized too late that his photo had been taken with a surprised look as he held a glass of alcohol.

Chapter 21

Brendan brought the bullet to the lab the next day and when he carefully opened the handkerchief, Clyde's eyes lit up at the prospect of a possible clue.

"Did you find this at the site?" he asked.

"No. Some kind soul left it in a beautiful blue box at the Burnside home last night a tad before supper was served. It put the kibosh on what promised to be a jolly evening with my fiancée and her family."

"I'm sorry to hear that. Who was it intended for?"

"That's a perplexing question. It could have been a warning for Amanda, who has done some investigating on this case on her own for a private client. Or it may have been for Louisa, who is Rob Worley's girlfriend."

"Or it could have been for you. Or her parents."

"What does her family have to do with anything?"

"That's the point. Scare everyone. You forget I spent most of my working life in Chicago. The gangsters there don't spare anyone if they're serious about getting you to back off." He paused. "Sorry, I didn't mean to be so blunt. But I'll take a look at it."

Brendan followed him over to the black slate-topped lab table in the middle of the room where his black cast iron microscope was mounted. He put a white cotton glove on his left hand and picked up the bullet.

"Let's just see if there is anything on it."

"What—like my initials?"

"That would be interesting," Clyde said rotating it under the scope.

He walked over to a table that abutted the wall, pulled out a jar and brush, and swept it over the bullet. Then back at the microscope he examined it from all angles."

"Nope. Clean. Lucky for you. It's a thirty-eight, though."

"Thought so. I'll put it in evidence for all the good that will do. Thanks."

Brendan returned to his office, picked up a pencil and drummed on the desktop with the eraser end while he thought. Then he made a list of all the possible suspects connected to the murder of the Mayor along with possible motivations. Considering how convoluted things had become, it was a long list. There were political issues to consider, moral issues for others, financial gain and perhaps just wanting someone who was an obstacle out of the way.

BRENDAN OUT down the pencil and took up his fountain pen. While he was scribbling his list with such speed that the ink was splattering from his pen, Mayor Carmichael was nursing a hangover in his office with a large glass of tomato juice.

Henry came in without knocking. "Hair of the dog works better, you know." He handed his boss a manila envelope and left.

"What now?" There was a Council meeting later in the day and he had no time for games.

He opened the envelope to see an eight- by ten-inch photo of himself looking like a deer in the headlights holding a glass that was half full. A note was attached. 'Call me. Selby.'

Carmichael closed his eyes and wished just then he had a bottle of bourbon in his desk drawer as many men did. Anything to get through this day. The group that had lobbied so hard to put further restrictions on operating hours for establishments serving alcohol had let him know they would be at the meeting in full force. He gulped down the rest of the tomato juice and picked up the telephone and dialed Selby's number.

"Good morning, Your Honor. I hope you're well."

"I've been better."

Selby chuckled. "I think, in light of recent events, you might want to postpone the vote on the ordinance."

"I can't do that. There will be a full house this afternoon. They're already annoyed that the item was taken off the agenda once."

"I can tell you that more than half of that full house will be the proprietors of some of Boston's best restaurants, clubs and watering holes, not to mention some folks who aren't in our membership because they can't afford the dues. All the Mom-and-Pop taverns have got wind of what's going on. They'll be there along with bartenders and waiters and waitresses. This is the livelihood of thousands in our community."

Carmichael sighed.

"Or we can just release that photo to the Boston Globe and all the other papers in the city and watch the fun."

"All right. All right. Here's the compromise," the Mayor said.

"No compromise," Selby said.

"Wait, wait. This will work. Since there will be so many people there from opposing sides on this issue, I'll recommend that we set up a committee to review the pros and cons of the ordinance and task them with coming up with modifications. We'll give them ninety days or something, and people will have calmed down by then. And we'll be into the summer season with fewer meetings and people out of town on vacation. In the meantime, your folks and the other folks will have plenty of time to meet with each Council Member and make their case. Who do you think most elected officials will side with when they realize the economic issue at stake?"

"Seeing as there is an election for some in the fall, that sounds like a good idea."

"Let me make myself clear. I understand the issue of drunk drivers at all hours and the notion that people could be encouraged to drink more than they can handle, but we must balance that with the livelihood of the people in the food and beverage industry."

"Well said, Mayor. We will be there in great numbers later today. And I'm sure you'll make good on your compromise." Selby hung up.

Carmichael cursed the man, but then he thought he had handled a difficult situation well. He would hand-pick the committee, which would assuage the supporters of the restrictions and balance it with some of the more well-known restaurateurs. The latter group could produce numbers showing how the sales tax of their businesses supported so much of the City's budget. The restrictors could point to moral objections, but in the end, the Council Members would see that the almighty dollar would win the day. Besides, the Food and Beverage Association folks would be the ones to donate to the upcoming election campaigns. He still had a bit of a headache, but he felt better about the upcoming meeting and tore up the speech that he had previously written.

Henry knocked on the door and came in without waiting to hear if he was welcome.

"You know I worked for O'Hara on every campaign and during his terms as Mayor. We've got to have a close relationship. So, let's cut out the crap of knocking and the honorifics."

Carmichael just stared.

"Here's the thing. Miss Johnstone out there doesn't have a clue about what working for a politician entails. She can type and she's pretty. Okay. But that doesn't go far enough in this arena. She has no idea who she's talking to on the telephone or which people to block from getting through to you. Send her back to the secretarial pool for the other Council Members. They'll be thrilled. And it will be easier on her. I want Mrs. Derwin back. She knows everybody who's anybody in this city. You won't be sorry."

Carmichael thought a moment. "Okay. But you're the one who's going to make all the arrangements."

"Fine with me, boss." Henry turned to go and stopped. He faced the Mayor and said, "Another thing. Bill, Paul and I are all appointees. I think we deserve a fifteen percent raise."

"What? I can't do that!"

"Of course, you can. You have a discretionary fund. It will come out of that. And my new title will be Chief of Staff. After all, you're having me deal with the other staff—hiring and reassigning—as well as other messy situations that may come up. I served Mayor O'Hara very well in that capacity."

"All right. Make the changes. Put in the paperwork for the salary adjustments. Then get out of here."

"Absolutely, boss," Henry said.

ALTHOUGH LOUISA WAS QUARANTINED, or under house arrest, as she put it, once her father and Amanda had left for work the next day and her mother was walking Cromwell, she went to her father's study and called Rob.

"Where are you?" he asked.

"At home. Forever."

"Oh, dear. That sounds bad."

"Don't be angry but I blurted about the engagement last night," she said, chewing on her finger.

"How did it go?"

"The usual drama, hysterics and crying," she said.

"And what about your mother?"

"Very funny. Brendan was here and I told him how I was at the club with you the entire time. It seemed to click something in his brain and I think we'll get you out of this jam."

"You, too, I suppose," Rob said, sounding hopeful.

"I'm the one you should feel sorry for. I'm locked up in a tower."

"You'd better grow your hair quickly if you want to be rescued, my Rapunzel."

"Actually, I have a better idea."

HAVING FINISHED HIS LIST, Brendan called Amanda and asked her to come to his office as soon as she could. He then found Dominic and sat him down to show him the chart he had compiled.

"Let's make sure Amanda is here first and we'll untangle this mess once and for all."

They didn't have long to wait as she was anxious to be done with the uncertainty about Rob's future.

"That's incredible!" she said, looking at the list of names and the adjoining possible motivations. "You usually gather everybody in person to talk through this."

"In this case, we've got some folks who would rather not face the inquisition. And frankly, seeing as how the Chief is my boss and the new Mayor is his boss, it would be career suicide to even suggest it."

"Good point," Dominic said with a smirk.

"Let's begin with the Chief. He seems to have had a close relationship with Mayor O'Hara. They were aligned in their public statements about crime and not pushing any more restrictions on clubs and bars," Brendan said.

"We even saw them in the same private room at the Oasis," Amanda said for Dominic's benefit. "They probably wanted to keep things private, but the singer and the band were so good that they came out to listen and we saw them."

"Several people mentioned that the late Mayor seemed a little out of it toward the end of the evening and Clyde found that someone had made sure that he was. But did you notice anything odd, Amanda?"

"All I saw were a bunch of men grinning at the performance. I think the singer's dress had something to do with it. Actually, I'd only seen the Mayor a few times in person, so I'm hardly the judge of what was normal and what was not."

"The Fire Marshal was there, too, and he was cagey about who the two constituents in the room were," Dominic said. "I don't see a motive there." Brendan ran a line through the Fire Marshal's name.

"The Chief seemed vague about them, too. Curious," Brendan said. "But I can't see a motive for him." He ran a line through the Chief's name. "I know we can't discount O'Hara's family and that is another reason I didn't want to gather everyone here. The poor widow has been through enough."

Amanda looked back and forth between the two men. "She might have been through more than you know." She paused. "I don't put much store in rumors, but the word is that he wasn't the most faithful of husbands."

"One particular woman?"

"The term 'womanizer' was used, implying possibly more than one fling. Not a mistress and secret child in a separate household. As far as was said."

"I don't know which would be more difficult to trace: one person or a bunch of women."

"Again, it's just a rumor," Amanda said.

"Reliable source?" Brendan asked.

"Very."

"Okay, then the widow's got a motive," Dominic said. He put a check mark next to her name.

"How reasonable is it that Mrs. O'Hara got a gun, went out at whatever hour of the night or morning and shot her husband? She may have known where he was, but she couldn't possibly have spiked his drink. That's not how women kill their husbands," Amanda said.

The two men looked at her in surprise.

"I've been reading up on domestic murders and men typically strangle or beat their wives. Women love to use poison."

Brendan and Dominic exchanged glances and gulped.

"Let's not forget about Kenny Deegan," Brendan said, once recovered from his fiancée's comments. "He's always been one hair's breadth away from serious danger. Not happening to him but causing it."

"He and the Mayor didn't get along, so I've heard," Dominic said. "The old man was always bailing him out of some scrape or another."

"But O'Hara did get him a job and I figure he subsidized the apartment, too. Not to mention a swell car," Brendan said. "He said he was moving back in with his mother, whether out of sympathy or to lend support or to get a better view of the financial position his mother is now in."

"Was there life insurance? Or a death benefit since he died in office?" Dominic asked.

"Excellent questions. Is the house paid off? Could you try to follow up on that? Perhaps not by asking her directly. Maybe one of his former staff could tell us about the City pension. I don't know how we can discreetly find out about the life insurance."

"I have some contacts that could help," Amanda said.

"Maybe there's been a large bank deposit in her account? But we don't have authorization to peek at her finances as I do when a husband or wife requests it," Amanda said.

"Another loose end, I'm afraid," Brendan said. "I don't want to seem prejudiced against Kenny, but he's always been a bad penny—hey, that rhymes—and we need to keep him on the active list."

"Now we're getting into the political arena. He and Carmichael did not get along. There was some business about the ordinance where they were on opposite sides of the issue."

"Is that enough to murder someone?" Dominic asked. "We're not in a banana republic here. Unless there's a lot of money at stake. I've got to tell you, the night of the murder when I went to use Worley's phone, he was digging all this cash out of his safe. It was a big bag of money! I mean big. On the way to the station, he put it in the night deposit chute at the bank. If he makes that much on a good night, he must be a millionaire."

The two men looked at Amanda for confirmation.

"I don't know anything about his finances. I always assumed that José Guzmán was the major owner but Louisa tole me Rob bought him out," she said.

"That's serious dough," Dominic said.

"But what has Rob got against O'Hara? The late Mayor intercepted an ordinance which would have cut down on the profits of the Oasis. That suggests Rob was a supporter, and killing O'Hara would have been the stupidest thing to do. And even if he wanted to, why in the world would he stage it in his own parking lot?" Amanda asked. Then she added, "I know that I'm not the most objective of participants here, but he's a smart man who has come up from a less than ideal background. He's found it hard to get where he is and I doubt he would endanger that by committing such a pointless crime."

"Agreed," Dominic said.

"Let's move on," Brendan said. "Carmichael seems to have had political differences with O'Hara, but we have no evidence he was at the scene. How could he be seen at a nightclub when he projects himself as a teetotaler?"

"Did he ever make threats against O'Hara?"

"That's not how politicians work," Brendan said. "They're more subtle."

"What if Carmichael or one of the other Council Members persuaded someone to spike the Mayor's drink to make him seem drunk? To discredit him?"

"Interesting," Brendan said.

"In the hopes that he would get in his car to go home and either crash or injure someone or himself?" Amanda continued. "How would that look in the newspapers? That would support the people who wanted to put restrictions on late service."

"Very good! Are we back to the two mysterious 'constituents' whose names nobody seems to remember?"

"Maybe that was someone's intention but killing him would be pointless. It doesn't make sense," Amanda said.

"Maybe the two things—the drugging and the shooting—are unconnected," Dominic said.

"Let's take a break," Brendan said. "There's coffee in the kitchen."

Dominic said behind his hand to Amanda, "It's been there since this morning. I would advise against it."

"I'll be back in a few minutes," Amanda said, knowing that there was only one women's bathroom in the station and a long walk to get to it. As she washed her hands, she thought how nothing made sense with this case. There didn't seem to be a logical motive unless the intent was not to kill the Mayor, particularly, but to discredit Rob. And who would want to do that?

When they resumed, she shared her thoughts. "Who wants to see Rob put away forever? Do you think there is some enemy from the past who has heard of his good fortune and seeks revenge?"

"I know so little about his past. When you think of it, he is perfectly charming and loquacious, but I still don't know anything about him."

"A man of mystery."

"What about José? Do you think he regretted selling his investment in the club?" Amanda asked.

"If he wanted to buy it back with funds from his family in Florida, that would be understandable. If they still have funds. But to go to that extreme to kill the Mayor? No. It would reflect badly on José and he's already got enough hurdles as a foreigner here."

"What do you think about the alcohol restrictors? There are so many of them and they were disappointed when Mayor O'Hara took it off the agenda."

"What about that Symington guy?" Dominic asked. "He seems like a real zealot. I've been to his place, remember? A strange guy. Claims to be an inventor but couldn't say what. Rather, he wouldn't say what. He also wouldn't confirm if he had been at home that night or not.

Listen! I've got a theory. What if this wily inventor figured out a way to have a bullet fired from a distance and nobody could trace the origin?"

"He said inventor, not magician," Brendan commented. "And what about drugging the Mayor?"

"Maybe that had nothing to do with his death," Dominic persisted.

"We've talked about just about everybody except the Morellis and the Russos," Brendan said.

"Since the Mayor was talking about law and order and crime, maybe they sought retaliation."

"Wouldn't killing the City's most important official prove the point of a need to curb crime?" Amanda asked.

They were silent for a few minutes as they looked at Brendan's chart with the check marks and crossed-out names.

"We heard about the events of that night from Louisa and what she saw from the window as she looked over the activity in the club. But I think I need to talk to Rob again to see if his account corroborates her story." He looked at his list of contacts and called the Oasis.

"Oasis Club, may I help you?" a man answered.

"This is Halloran. Is Rob Worley there?" he asked.

"Let me check." The receiver was put down and the man was gone for a few minutes, returning a bit out of breath. "Sorry, he's left. I didn't see him go but someone said he left about a half hour ago."

"Do you know where he went?"

"He said he was going to see his attorney. If so, he'll be back in an hour or so to get ready for the evening."

"Thanks," Brendan said and looked at the other two.

"May I use the phone?" Amanda asked.

She dialed her home number and her mother picked up.

"Hello. Can Louisa come to the phone? We have a few follow-up questions to ask her."

"Oh, I've been out with Cromwell. Let me go see."

Amanda waited for the time it would take her mother to go upstairs and check her bedroom and bathroom. She came back to the phone. "She's not upstairs. Let me ask Simona and Mary if they've seen her go out. Which she is not supposed to do!" Another few minutes and her mother returned to the call.

"Cook said a car pulled up to the back of the house and Louisa ran down the stairs and got in. Cook was so distracted that she couldn't tell me if she recognized the car or the driver. Do you think she's been kidnapped? Shall I call the police?"

"Mother, I'm here in Brendan's office. I'll tell him and we'll try to figure out what's going on. Call Daddy and have him come home to be with you."

Amanda hung up the receiver and said, "Louisa's gone! The Morellis or the Russos must have taken her."

Chapter 22

"Why do you say that?"

"Cook told my mother that Louisa went down the back stairs and into a car."

"Of her own will?"

"Well, I don't know!" Amanda said in a panic. "We have to find her."

"How can we do that if we don't know where she went and with whom?"

Amanda collapsed into a chair. "I'm sure the gangs are behind this. The bullet, remember? Maybe she's been lured into a car under false pretenses to exonerate Rob."

"Let's think this through. What have the two gangs got to do with your sister and Rob?

When I asked him if he was paying Morelli protection, he acknowledged that there was a bit of a deal. He lets them have a private room and provides drinks in return for some oversight from those folks. It would stand to reason that, while the deal could be more lucrative for the Morellis, I can't imagine that they would murder the Mayor. It would ruin their privileges there and possibly close down the club for good."

"What about the Russos?" Dominic asked.

Keeping in mind that Dominic's cousin was employed by some branch of the Morellis, he had to consider the suggestion carefully.

"What are you thinking?"

"What if the Russos wanted to take over the club? What better way than to discredit the previous owner? If Rob gets convicted, he can no longer own the liquor license or be in any way connected to the business. The ABC Commission is very strict about that. Get rid of Rob by pinning the murder on him and the club is essentially up for grabs."

"I want to talk to Vince again and get his side of the story. Call him up and get him in here as soon as possible."

Dominic left and Brendan said to Amanda, "I think it would be best if you step away now."

Her chin went up in defiance.

"This is starting to look entirely like a gang situation and I can't have you involved." He took her hand. "Please, go home to your parents, who are probably sick with worry. I have a feeling Louisa will show up soon, safe and sound."

Amanda rushed into his arms for an embrace. "All right. Just this one time," she admonished him before leaving.

Vince made it to the station within a half-hour, wide-eyed and apprehensive.

"What's going on?" he asked Brendan.

"Just sit. We need to go over the events of the night the Mayor was shot. Something doesn't fit."

Vince, still in his overcoat, sat leaning forward with elbows on his knees and focused his dark eyes on Brendan.

"A few witnesses have come forward since we last talked."

"Who?"

"I can't tell you that, but we're closing in on the perpetrator."

"The Morellis? I heard they have hit men who specialize in that sort of thing."

"No, I think it's someone closer to home," Brendan said.

Vince looked very odd at that moment.

"Are you okay?" Brendan asked.

"It must have been something I ate. Where's the bathroom?"

Brendan yanked him out of the chair before he vomited on the floor and pushed him toward the door. Go right, then first right down the hall. Can't miss it."

Vince flew around the corner, to the right and out of sight.

Brendan reconsidered what to tell Vince about the witness information. The neighbor across the street from the Oasis was safe—all Brendan had to do was say that 'somebody' saw and heard something.

The phone rang and he picked it up.

"You got home fast," he said.

"After Cook described the car, it turns out it was Rob's. He usually parks in the street so she's never seen it. Or him, for that matter, since he's not been here often."

"Do you think they've gone to his house?"

"I don't know. I don't even know where his house is!"

"Vince is here. I'm sure he knows. I'll get the address from him."

"Wait, I'm coming, too. Just swing by here before you go to Rob's house."

Brendan agreed, thinking that they were not in any danger because he assumed that the couple had either checked into a hotel or left the city. Or maybe Rob had a bolt hole for just such occasions. It had been some minutes since Vince had gone. Brendan went to the bathroom that had several stalls and, pushing each one open, found nobody there.

Brendan cursed to himself for being so stupid, ran to his office for coat and hat and hurried to the front entrance.

"Hey, what did you do to that guy? He went tearing out of here," the officer at the desk said to him.

"Yeah, I know. He's got something to hide."

When he got out to the street, he looked in both directions but Vince was gone, run off to wherever he had parked his car and then—where? He trotted to his own car in the parking lot and took off at a fast clip, speeding through several yellow lights and getting to Beacon Hill in record time. He parked out front and ran up the steps to see Amanda opening the door to him.

"I found the address."

"Where?"

"Telephone book, of course. Although it was listed under L. Robert Worley."

"Before we go, see if you can find Vince Renard's address. If he's got a phone."

She rushed back into the hallway to the small table that had a telephone on it and the directory on a shelf below. "Vincent Renard? Here it is. It's in Bay Village. Why?"

"I think he's our man."

They got into his car and he started driving.

"Why do you say that?"

"When I started questioning him, he said he felt sick and left the room. In reality, he ran out of the station. He either knows who did it or he did it himself."

"Why?"

"His silence might have been traded for the possibility or promise of managing the club. Not owning it, of course. I suspect he colluded with one of the gangs."

"Don't you think we ought to check Rob's house for Louisa?"

"It's in the other direction and, if she's there, she's perfectly safe. And if he doesn't think it's a safe place, they're somewhere else and they'll show up when they do feel safe."

Brendan turned onto Stuart Street, then Arlington and finally Winchester and glanced at the paper with Vince's address on it.

"There it is," Amanda said.

He pulled over and double-parked. "Stay in the car. Here are the keys. You can move it if necessary."

"Be careful," she said, wanting to go along with him but suspecting she would be more of a hinderance. She kept the motor running and got into the driver's seat in case the man escaped and they had to pursue him.

Brendan walked up the inside stairwell of the two-story house as fast as he could manage without making excessive noise. There were two apartments on the top floor and from behind the door of one of them was the noise of things being dropped and dragged amid rapid footsteps. He paused, deciding whether he ought to knock, but before he got the chance, the door was flung open and he and Vince were eye to eye.

"Get out of my way!" Vince shouted and pushed at Brendan with a large suitcase he held in front of his body, flinging Brendan to the floor and jamming his foot in the banister.

"Stop! Police!" Brendan yelled as he yanked his foot free from between two spindles of the banister. He managed to pull himself up and heard Vince flying down the stairs, crashing into a baby carriage parked at the bottom, yet pushing his way past to the entry.

Brendan ran down the stairs two steps at a time and could see Vince through the front door's glass, tearing across the small grass lawn and down the street.

Amanda saw the escape, put the car into gear and followed Vince who was oblivious to her. He opened the driver's side of his car clumsily, looking over his shoulder to see the detective coming after him on the sidewalk, flung the suitcase into the passenger seat and started the car. Just as he was about to pull out, another car came up beside him, blocking his exit.

"Get out of the way!" he screamed at the woman whose car stayed in place.

He honked the horn. "Move! It's an emergency!"

She said nothing and just looked at him.

Vince finally knew who it was in the other car. "You!" he screamed and looked back to see Brendan only two car lengths behind him. Taking a risk he felt well worth it, Vince turned the steering wheel and stepped on the gas, mashing the front left fender of Brendan's car. The sound of broken headlights shattered the air, but he was trapped.

Brendan opened the driver's side and hauled Vince out. "You're under arrest, pal. And you or your buddies are going to pay for the damage to my car!" He pulled a set of handcuffs from his overcoat pocket, yanked the man's hands behind his back and clicked the cuffs shut.

"I'm not saying anything. You don't have anything on me," Vince shouted.

"We'll see about that. You're coming down to the station and this time not sneaking out. You're going to tell me how this whole scheme was hatched and who's behind it."

"I'm not saying anything."

AS IT TURNED OUT, Vince talked a lot, with Brendan and Dominic listening to his tales.

"First, let me say that when you called me in to the station, you threatened me."

"I certainly did not," Brendan said.

"You said you would break both my kneecaps if I didn't confess."

Brendan looked at Dominic. "Nice try. I don't think I would know how to break someone's kneecaps. With the ruler I have in my desk? Come on, you can do better than that."

"We have a witness who saw you in the Oasis after closing," Dominic said.

"I was in the club from opening until closing. And after the club closed, me and the waiters did the last clearing up and I had a smoke with the boss until it was time to leave. It was when I went out to the parking lot and saw not just Rob's car, but my car and another with someone sitting in the driver's seat but the engine wasn't running. It looked like the Mayor's car and I thought maybe he had too much to drink and passed out. But he had been shot."

"By you."

"Not by me! I don't own a gun. The last time I shot anything was with a toy rifle at a carnival."

"Here's what I think. I think you saw how much money Rob pulled in and got the idea to put yourself in his position. Although he wasn't just the manager, he had bought out Guzmán some time ago and he owned the place. You didn't have the cash to buy Rob out—even if he wanted to sell—which he didn't. But if you ran the place, you'd be making much more money than you currently earn. You scoped out the Morellis and thought about making a deal with them, but they were happy with the relationship as it stood. They got free booze, respect and possibly protection money, as well. They were regulars at a high-class club and they didn't want to ruin a good thing. But the Russos were hungry to turn the tables on the rival gang. If they created a situation where it looked like the current owner was responsible for major crimes at his business, then the liquor license would be up for grabs. And better yet, if he were set up as the primary suspect and he had attorney fees to pay and then was convicted, the club would sell at a rock-bottom price."

"That's when the Russos would make a generous offer for the place and put in a manager of their own choosing. You. Perfectly placed, you knew how everything ran, knew the staff, knew a little about the books and were hungry to be the guy to tally up the receipts at the end of the night and put a handful of cash in your pocket while you were at it. Everybody knows that people who operate on a cash basis always take a little extra home every night, right?"

"I'm not saying anything," Vince said.

"It was when Rob went upstairs after only you and he were still there. You popped out quickly, shot the Mayor, whose drink you had spiked earlier, then ran down the street and dumped the gun in the ashcan and came back quietly. Then, when Rob came back down, you chewed the fat with the boss, cool as a cucumber. After a smoke, you left as if it was for the first time that night, spotted the Mayor's car and himself in it, and came back in and reported that something horrible had happened. You went back out with Rob, approached the car more carefully and the two of you returned inside to call us."

"And I want an attorney."

"I'm sorry to say the best criminal defense attorney in town is already defending Rob Worley. But I'm sure the court can provide you with some young guy, just out on his own, who is looking to cut his teeth on an interesting case."

Chapter 23

The District Attorney was thrilled to have someone in custody and he was sure he would eventually spill the beans on the Russos. If he lived to tell the tale, that is.

The search for Louisa and Rob ended when they turned up the next day, acting surprised that anyone had noticed their absence. They sat in the Burnsides' sitting room with her parents, who were still angry with her sudden disappearance.

"We just needed to get away from the pressures of all this business," Louisa said dismissively.

Her parents stared at her nonchalance. After a few moments, Rob spoke up calmly.

"We drove to Thomas, Connecticut, and got married."

The Burnsides, including Brendan and Amanda, exchanged glances.

"We asked Rob's attorney about the issue of a wife testifying against her husband. We decided to play it safe and protect him by taking this step. Which we were going to do anyway, as you know," Louisa said.

Mr. and Mrs. Burnside were shocked into silence.

"Congratulations to you both," Brendan said. "Although that is a moot point now that we have in custody the perfidious Vince, who did the deed and dumped the gun in a nearby ashcan. Although he will likely continue to maintain it was somebody else." He stood and held out the glass of sherry and the others followed suit. "Long life and happiness."

After she had regained her composure, Mrs. Burnside said, "Oh, Louisa. I had hoped for a lavish society wedding for you. And a spectacular wedding dress of your own design."

"I'm sorry, Mother, but things were getting very nasty and we had to act. I'm so glad that Brendan put two and two together and focused on the real motivations behind this terrible crime."

"I was surprised to read that Mayor Carmichael, who was so strongly behind shortening open hours of clubs, bars, restaurants and taverns, decided to back away with a long period of study and input," Rob said.

Mr. Burnside finally had relaxed enough to chuckle. "He's got a committee and they'll get so worn down by the process of appointment, the months of meetings without a quorum, the interminable proposals and those who are for or against, that it will die from exhaustion."

"Or the Food and Beverage Association will make enough donations to the campaigns of those Council Members that it will no longer be an issue," Brendan said.

"But back to the wedding. Can't we at least have a party for the two of you?" Mrs. Burnside said. Her husband scowled at the notion.

"That would be lovely, Mrs. Burnside," Rob said.

"And I have another suggestion," Brendan began, looking at Amanda. "Why don't we make it a double wedding and reception?"

"Where? How?" Amanda asked since she thought the issue had been far from resolved.

"We'll get my brother, Father Patrick, to officiate alongside the minister of your church."

"That's highly unorthodox," Mr. Burnside said in his lawyerly tone.

"I was thinking that it could be considered a step toward including everybody rather than having to make a choice. I know my brother would agree to it. You'd just have to consult your minister." Brendan took Amanda's hand and looked into her eyes with a smile. "What do you say?"

"I say yes," Amanda said, leaning over to kiss him.

"What about the children's religious upbringing?" Mrs. Burnside asked.

"Now, now, we're not there yet, Margaret. One step at a time. One step at a time."

What's Next?

A double wedding, a new home and everything seems to be settling down.
Until autumn when Amanda and Brendan are invited to a costume party.
And a

MURDER AT THE HALLOWEEN PARTY

Sign up for my newsletter for more titles:

www.Andreas-books.com

Reviews help readers discover my books, so feel free to leave some stars.

Thank you! Happy Reading,
Andrea

COPYRIGHT

© ANDREA KRESS 2025

Printed in Dunstable, United Kingdom